BY JEN BESSER AND SHANA FESTE

Dirty Diana

Diana in Love

Diana Says Yes

Diana Says Yes

A Dirty Diana Novel

Jen Besser and Shana Feste

THE DIAL PRESS

New York

The Dial Press
An imprint of Random House
A division of Penguin Random House LLC
1745 Broadway, New York, NY 10019
randomhousebooks.com
penguinrandomhouse.com

A Dial Press Trade Paperback Original

Copyright © 2025 by Jennifer Besser and Quiet Girl Productions

Penguin Random House values and supports copyright. Copyright fuels creativity, encourages diverse voices, promotes free speech, and creates a vibrant culture. Thank you for buying an authorized edition of this book and for complying with copyright laws by not reproducing, scanning, or distributing any part of it in any form without permission. You are supporting writers and allowing Penguin Random House to continue to publish books for every reader. Please note that no part of this book may be used or reproduced in any manner for the purpose of training artificial intelligence technologies or systems.

THE DIAL PRESS is a registered trademark and the colophon is a trademark of Penguin Random House LLC.

LIBRARY OF CONGRESS CATALOGING-IN-PUBLICATION DATA
Names: Besser, Jen, author. | Feste, Shana, 1976– author.
Title: Diana says yes / Jen Besser and Shana Feste.
Description: New York, NY: The Dial Press, 2025. | Series: Dirty Diana; 3
Identifiers: LCCN 2025014512 (print) | LCCN 2025014513 (ebook) |
ISBN 9780593447703 (trade paperback; acid-free paper) |
ISBN 9780593447710 (ebook)
Subjects: LCGFT: Erotic fiction. | Novels.
Classification: LCC PS3602.E7828 D54 2025 (print) | LCC PS3602.E7828 (ebook) |
DDC 813/.6—dc23/eng/20250404
LC record available at https://lccn.loc.gov/2025014512
LC ebook record available at https://lccn.loc.gov/2025014513

Printed in the United States of America on acid-free paper

1st Printing

BOOK TEAM: Production editor: Cindy Berman • Managing editor: Rebecca Berlant • Production manager: Maggie Hart • Copy editor: Laurie McGee

Book design by Debbie Glasserman

The authorized representative in the EU for product safety and compliance is Penguin Random House Ireland, Morrison Chambers, 32 Nassau Street, Dublin D02 YH68, Ireland.
https://eu-contact.penguin.ie.

For our best friends. All of them.

Nature repeats herself, or almost always does:
repeat, repeat, repeat; revise, revise, revise.

—ELIZABETH BISHOP, "North Haven"

PART ONE

Dallas, Texas

Chapter One

Oliver and I used to sit as far apart as possible on the love seat in our therapist's office. We were careful never to touch each other as we excavated our marriage. Week after week, we showed up to see Miriam, dutifully, sometimes passively, never quite happily. It's strange to be back now, sitting so close to my husband that I feel his thigh against mine. When one of us shifts, an electricity passes between us. We're like lovers wishing to be alone, like maybe then we'd tear our clothes off and make love right here beneath Miriam's shelves of purple geodes and self-improvement books, to the tinkling sound of her zen fountain that drifts in from the waiting room.

"What about dating?" Miriam's pencil hovers above her notebook. Her hair is styled so differently than the last time we were here. It now reaches her shoulders in wavy layers, just like her clothing—layers upon layers of purposefully rumpled linen. There's new jewelry, too, an unfamiliar pink beaded necklace and another stack of silver rings.

"Dating?" I steal a glance at Oliver, hoping he might take this one, but his eyes are on the ceiling, his mouth twisted in deep thought.

"I reconnected with an old friend. Jasper." Old friend? "And we dated." I don't know how to describe Jasper—or our relationship—in this room. Or maybe in any room. And saying his name out loud in front of Oliver still feels cruel, even though he's been seeing someone too. "And Oliver was in a relationship with a woman named Katherine." After a too-long beat I feel compelled to add, "She's very nice. A really wonderful person."

"But those relationships are over. For both of us." Oliver lays his hand on mine. A warm tingle runs up my arm. Miriam jots something in her notebook. Should I explain that I had given Oliver plenty of space to end things with Katherine? And that once they'd broken up, Oliver and I kept things perfectly polite for weeks? Even in my head it sounds too much like I'm trying to impress my therapist. So I don't explain how November rolled into the holidays, loaded with expectations and family traditions, which felt like way too precarious of a time to dip a toe in and risk confusing things for our daughter, Emmy. And if we weren't back together, there was no reason to tell Oliver about Dirty Diana—even though the website is growing and steadily building a fan base, with my business partner, Petra, constantly coming up with new ways to expand. So instead, Oliver and I kept things the way they'd been for months—living apart, shuttling Emmy back and forth between us.

Only recently, our hugs have lasted too long. And a kiss meant for my cheek had brushed against my lips. Last weekend, as we tucked Emmy into bed, my hand found Oliver's, and while she drifted off to sleep, my heart pounded in my chest so loudly I thought for sure he could hear it.

"I see." Miriam flips back a page in her notebook, then back again.

Her expression is stunningly, annoyingly neutral. "But what I meant is, what about dating each other?"

A nervous guffaw escapes us both, startled and weirdly synced.

"Oliver and me?"

"Date? Like strangers?"

"We're way beyond the dating stage," I say with a laugh.

"It's been a million years," Oliver adds. "And a wedding. And a baby."

"Who's not even a baby anymore."

"Right. Exactly."

As Oliver and I list all the reasons the two of us can't date, Miriam leans back in her chair, hands folded in her lap. Everything about her body language suggests she now realizes she must zoom way out and explain things more slowly to the dummies on her couch. I should find this condescending, but it's oddly comforting. Maybe it's her easy smile or the way her loose linen pants make you feel as if she's waiting patiently for a summer breeze.

"Why don't you take me back to that day. What happened after Oliver came to you and said"—she glances at her notes—"'I want to handcuff you to the sink.'"

It was early November then. Unseasonably hot, even for Texas, but there Oliver was, planting zinnias for me in our front yard.

"Diana?" Miriam asks. "What was your response? To Oliver?"

Heat rises up my neck and flushes my cheeks, the same way it did that day. And just like then, here I am now, searching for the right words and floundering. "I was . . . surprised."

"Okay. What else?"

"I liked the idea. In theory." I cringe at my robotic answer. "The problem was it all just felt so far away. From where we were at the time. Like the idea could *occur* to us but didn't belong to us. Does that make sense?" Of course it doesn't. It's a load of mismatched socks tumbling from my tongue.

"Did you accept Oliver's invitation?"

"No."

"Did you reject it?"

"I invited him in. For iced tea." My face burns a deeper shade of pink. "It was such a hot day."

"And Oliver? How did it feel for you? In the moment?"

"Unbelievable. To say those words out loud. I'd been thinking about Diana and missing her so much." His tone is light but careful. We can both feel it—the way just talking about our sex lives is like a new entity has come into the room.

"I also liked hearing that he wanted us to be so adventurous. I wanted the handcuffs." I laugh again. "Sorry. It just sounds so funny, out of context." No one else is smiling along. I clear my throat. "But I was also very aware of what happened last time."

"Last time?" Miriam asks.

"When we had sex just after Oliver had moved out, I wanted it then too. But it wasn't right." Oliver flinches at the memory of us at his parents' party, sneaking upstairs to have sex and thinking it would be okay, fun even. It was awful, both of us reeling from the pain of our separation, Oliver's angry voice in my ear, harsh and unfamiliar. Instead of bringing us closer, the sex had left us lonely and far apart.

"I'm sorry." Oliver squeezes my hand.

"What was it, you think, that made it not right then?"

"We hadn't done the work," Oliver says. "It was a temporary fix."

"And now we're hoping . . ."

We're hoping you'll tell us this is a good idea.

Like two eager teenagers who have barely passed their driving tests, we've come asking to borrow your expensive car. Can you tell us getting back together is the right thing to do? Can I please let my husband tie me to the sink? Can we put all the ugliness behind us and move ahead? What do you say, Miriam?

"We're hoping to try again," Oliver says.

"It's a big decision. And one I can see excites the both of you."

Oliver and I have scooted so far forward we've adopted the cartoonish posture of audience members on the edge of our seats. "The marriage fantasy—your reconciliation—will always be on the table, so to speak. Don't be afraid to leave it there. While we do the work in here."

We have! We've left it there for months! Isn't it time to dust it off?

But what if it's not? What if this is just a passing moment? A fondness that has grown since we've been apart, that will be suffocated once we're back together. Suffocated by little digs, tiny annoyances, swallowed feelings, and waning desires.

As if reading my mind, Miriam adds, "I would like to see the both of you date first."

"You mean take it slow?" I think of all our recent lingering looks, the once casual hug goodbye now loaded with want.

"Yes. Take your time. Date."

"No sex?" Oliver asks.

Miriam holds our gaze. "Would you let someone tie you to a sink on the first date?"

I smile. Finally, someone else in the room cracking a joke—it's like I can breathe again.

Oliver's laugh is less relaxed. "I don't think I would ask."

"You two are turning over a new leaf in your relationship. And you need to create a safe foundation. Court each other. Rebuild that trust. Foreplay," she says, looking from me to Oliver and back again. "Emotional foreplay."

"For how much longer?" Oliver asks. "If you could be specific."

Miriam smiles at her A student. "There's no set schedule. But take it slow. You'll know when the time is right. Just like both of you know that now is not the right time."

"Right," we agree, while at the same time silently willing ourselves to be as wise as Miriam.

...

Oliver walks me to my car, his hands buried in the pockets of his jeans. It's a gray, late-February day, cool with an almost imperceptible drizzle. I wrap my thin cotton jacket closed.

There are only three cars in the parking lot today: Oliver's, a new baby-blue Ford pickup truck that comfortably sits two people not three; mine, a champagne-colored minivan he and I bought when Emmy was a baby, and when the possibility of us having a second child still lingered—never spoken about but always hanging around us, like a necklace you try on with every outfit but never leave the house in. By process of elimination, then, the sensible gray sedan is Miriam's. Often, in our therapy sessions last year, I tried to picture Miriam outside of work. A respite from all the heated arguments in that room, with all their yawning, resentment-filled pauses. Mostly, imagining Miriam's life was a cool washcloth against my fevered forehead. But sometimes, when I let myself really slip underwater and into despair, picturing Miriam's personal life wasn't comforting. It was terrifying. What if she's a real person and not a superhero who can save our sinking marriage?

In the end, she didn't save it. Oliver moved out and we've spent the last several months living apart. We gathered divorce attorney referrals like hot new restaurants recommendations. We dropped Emmy off at the other's place without small talk or eye contact because some days meeting Oliver's gaze was too painful, like staring directly into the sun.

But here we are now, hopeful and curious on a rainy February day. I sneak a glance at Oliver and catch a smirk. When he notices me looking, his smile blossoms. He gently knocks his shoulder into mine, and a jolt of electricity runs through me. The brush of his arm against mine. The excitement of having him close. I can't keep my own smile from spreading.

Maybe Miriam didn't fail after all. Maybe she is a superhero genius. Maybe that's not even her sedan.

The rain falls more steadily, in colder, fatter drops. "Well"—Oliver waits while I search for my keys instead of ducking into his truck—"Miriam was direct and perfectly clear." He tips his chin up to the gray sky. "Sounds to me like a hard yes re sex."

"Oh, definitely. She practically reached behind her back and produced the handcuffs."

I open my car door as Oliver touches my shoulder. "Diana. I really want to do this right. Even if it means slowly."

I lace my fingers through his. Neither of us moves an inch, despite the rain. "Me too."

"It's better for all of us. Especially for Emmy."

"Right."

Oliver rocks back on his heels and smiles. "Diana, would you like to go on a date with me?"

I smooth a wet curl from his forehead. I study his eyes, his full, rosy lips. For months, I've imagined what it would be like to kiss him again. And now I can think of nothing else. "I would like to go on a date with you. Yes."

Oliver quickly closes the distance between us. "Diana?" His lips nearly brush against mine. "I'm nervous. You're my beautiful wife."

His confession is both heartbreaking and exhilarating. I run my fingers through his wet hair and pull him closer. I press against the softness of his lips, tasting the rain and the salt on his skin. Our kiss is slow and tentative. And then the floodgates crash open and we kiss until I feel dizzy with this welcome, confusing sensation of kissing a man I know better than anyone, but who somehow feels totally unfamiliar.

Oliver steps back and smiles sheepishly. We're soaked by the rain but a warm shiver runs through me. "I have an hour before I have to meet with an electrician. Can I buy you a cup of coffee?"

We sit at the counter of a nearby diner. My breath is steady, and the flush has left Oliver's cheeks. We order coffee and share a day-old chocolate donut, and, outside, the rain never lets up. Our wet clothes drip onto the linoleum floor and Oliver keeps trying to mop up the rain with napkins so no one gets mad, which makes me laugh because it's so sweet and adorable and futile. And because laughing is like releasing the valve on the tension between us. I'm late for work but there is nowhere else I want to be.

Whoever sat at the counter before us has left behind their copy of *The New York Times* and we read it together, open before us, always in sync and ready to flip the page at the same time. It reminds me of us before Emmy, when we'd spend entire days reading together for hours.

We study the headlines, linger an extra beat on the real estate section, skim the sports pages, then pore over a piece on the continuing mystery of a missing tech mogul. We flip to the arts section and on the second page, I freeze.

Who Is Dirty Diana?

The headline runs beneath one of my paintings from the site. It's Andrea, who shared her fantasy months ago. She sits at a train window, a blurred landscape behind her. There is a short paragraph with a few hundred words describing Dirty Diana as an online space for erotic stories, run by a mysterious artist who interviews the women who share their fantasies on the site.

I hurriedly turn the page, nearly choking on my panic.

This couldn't be me. There is no way *The New York Times* is talking about me. I hurry to my feet. "I should really get going."

I expect Oliver to shoot me a confused look but he only glances at a missed call and sighs. "Yeah, me too."

"Mind?" I ask, and before he can answer I fold up the *Times* and tuck it beneath my arm.

Chapter Two

Through my windshield, I watch Oliver drive away, growing smaller and smaller. When he's completely out of sight, I flip open the paper.

WHO IS DIRTY DIANA?

Dirty Diana, the artist behind an erotic website made for women by women, prefers to stay anonymous. Scan the site for any one of the hand-painted stunners and listen to a spicy, unfiltered story.

I toss the paper onto the passenger seat. I think about calling L'Wren, my only true friend in Rockgate, and telling her everything about this morning so we can laugh together until it all starts to feel like it's happening to someone else. I would describe the way Oliver and I kissed and how I wish he had kissed me like that our entire marriage. And how minutes later I was almost outed by *The New York Times*. How I'm still too much of a wimp to tell him about the site because I believe it would lead him to pull away, right when things finally feel so good. Whenever I picture telling him everything, I flash back to the night, months ago, when I played one of the fantasies for him. His confused look. The argument we fell into. I didn't explain the site then. *How could I?* I tell myself now. *Moments later, he walked out the door.* But that's not why I keep stalling. If I share the site with him, and he still doesn't understand, neither of us would get over it. His disappointment in me would make me hate him, I think, so instead I've stayed quiet.

I imagine L'Wren's immediate response: "I cannot believe you haven't told him yet. This isn't something you fudge a little, like blaming a nose job on a deviated septum." Then once she'd gotten over the shock that he and I had made out, she'd tell me, "Honestly? You should write to all the women Oliver dated while you were separated. Send them a thank-you card for boosting his self-esteem. This is Texas. They'll appreciate it."

But what if she doesn't joke with me? Not being forthcoming about Dirty Diana with L'Wren is exactly what made *her* so angry with me. It caused the worst fight we've ever had. I'm trying to give her space while also needing her to forgive me. I dial her number, then, nervous she'll send me straight to voicemail, I hang up. Instead I call in sick to work at the wealth management firm and drive straight to the Dirty Diana offices.

Our space is in a state of constant construction. In the last few months, Petra has built out a soundproofed studio and walled offices, plenty of room for Liam, L'Wren's stepson who helped me build the site, and Kirby, the intern he hired to work on the sound design. My good friend Alicia occasionally beams in from Santa Fe to help with editing the fantasies, and I come in on the evenings and weekends that Emmy is with Oliver. We have a nice rhythm going, with the goal of posting three new interviews a week, but my paintings are coming much slower. As of a couple weeks ago, we no longer have to find women to share their stories, they've been coming to us. We now have a fifty-person waiting list and a very sweet office manager, Lou, a retired librarian, to vet the fantasies first. "This was a really nasty batch," she'll tell me, tapping her hot pink nail on a stack of papers. And I'll gently remind her that there are no nasty fantasies. "Fine. At least let me spell-check them first."

Petra spends about a quarter of her time in Dallas and the rest of her time between Paris and everywhere else. When she is in town, she drops by and checks on us and feeds us helpful suggestions. She doesn't push too hard—except around marketing. "It's why I'm here," she reminds us.

When I arrive, Liam and Kirby are hanging around Lou's desk, reading *The New York Times* and wearing matching grins.

"They might not know who Dirty Diana is but we sure do," Liam says.

"Did you know about this?" I ask.

"I don't even think Petra knew about this."

"I'd love to take credit, but it wasn't me!" Petra calls from down the hall.

I follow the sound of her voice to her office. She feigns alarm at the sight of bedraggled me in her doorway. "Seriously, how hard is it raining?"

"Petra . . ." I sit across from her. "Something to tell me?"

"Yes, *of course* it was me. Please. Isn't it great? You are officially part of the zeitgeist, Diana."

I eye the desk between us, strewn with photos of me from the one and only photo shoot I've ever done. I try not to pick apart my crooked smile or the way my right eye always looks like it's at half-mast. I dislike the photos for looking both too much like me and not enough like me. And then feel annoyed at myself for caring so much. I pick up one of me overeagerly smiling into the camera and looking slightly deranged and slip it to the bottom of the pile.

"Maybe we send this one to the *Times* and solve the mystery for them?" Petra holds up a picture of me in our offices, painting near the window, and even though it was candid, to me it looks too posed.

"It's a nice piece, thank you. But is anyone actually curious who I am?"

"Now they are! First we create the mystery . . . and then we out you. It'll be a kick."

"Or"—I race to buy myself more time—"I out myself? At the perfect moment? Maybe tease things out a little longer?"

"No. I think *Vogue* should announce you."

"Sure." I laugh. "*Vogue*. Even better."

"I'm serious. They want a three-quarter shot." Her hand hovers over one of me unsmiling, my dark hair falling across my face. "They're going to be the first to use the image. Alongside a fun, getting-to-know-you Q&A. They already sent the questions."

"*Vogue?*"

"I'm good at my job, Diana. It's why I'm here."

"They want to feature me?"

"Well. Maybe not feature. More like intro. The *Times* piece was a bit of a favor and now *Vogue* is all in. It's perfect." Petra swivels her screen to show me an email. "They barely do in-person interviews anymore, and they certainly don't have a journalist at the ready in Rockgate. But these things are better in writing anyway. This way you can really think through all your answers." *And then run them by me,* I know she wants to add but doesn't, even though I'd be thrilled to have her edit my answers. Or even write them.

I skim the email, reading the first question aloud. "Where's your favorite place to wake up?" And then skipping the next several questions, all the way to the last one: "Tell us, what's your fantasy?"

"Don't worry too much about the actual answers. Just getting our name out there is a massive jump start."

"And when does all this really start? That people will know it's me?"

"When the piece runs, I guess. A couple months from now . . ." She studies my expression. "Diana. We talked about this. You were on board with moving ahead."

"I am. I'm so grateful. It's just starting to feel . . ."

"Quick? It's not."

"Petra."

"Tell me why it feels fast. And saying you're scared isn't an option."

"Because I still haven't told Oliver."

"Oh." An abrupt, single syllable, dripping in disappointment. But she kindly marches on, waving a hand. "The piece won't run for another couple months. But really, Diana, why wait?"

Alone in my office, I find a stack of notecards submitted by fans of the site, each one with a "micro-fantasy"—Petra's latest idea—to share online. I read the first one:

*I don't know the man massaging me. He's a total stranger in an unfamiliar but upscale spa. Crisp sheets beneath me, and the bed warmer is set to five. I've given my masseuse three easy-to-follow rules: 1. No talking. I don't care who he is or where he's from 2. He cannot fuck me. He can touch me anywhere he likes but **only** for my pleasure, never his. And 3. The massage must have a very happy ending. For me.*

I smile and tape the card to the wall. I read the next one, then the next. I pore over them with a familiar feeling of gratitude, admiring the collage and trying to focus while I hear Petra in my head. *Why wait?*

...

Saturday is my birthday, so I give myself the gift of sleeping in. Emmy and Oliver already FaceTimed me at 6 A.M. to sing happy birthday, and my head hit the pillow again as soon as we hung up. By eleven, I'm finally dressed and out the door.

I buy sunflowers to spruce up the guest room for Alicia. At the liquor store, I pick up a festive-looking bottle of vodka for us. And the entire time, I can't keep Petra's voice out of my head. She's right. I have to quit stalling and tell Oliver.

When I get home, I unlock the front door and enter the house in a fog, the whole time trying to decide if there's a version where Oliver doesn't get upset I've kept this secret from him.

"Surprise!" Alicia pops up from behind the couch, and my heart leaps into my throat.

"Alicia." In a split second, I go from scared to angry to delighted by the sight of her in my house, wearing a hat shaped like a wilted blue birthday cake with six floppy red candles.

"Happy birthday!" She wraps her arms around me and pulls me close.

"I thought I was picking you up at your dad's?"

"I drove up early so I could surprise you."

She studies a spot just over my right shoulder like she always does when she's lying.

"His new girlfriend is that awful?"

"She might be the worst one yet."

"Older or younger than you?" I take her by the hand and into the kitchen.

I grab us two glasses—the crystal Tom Collins glasses that were an anniversary gift from Oliver's mom—and rinse the dust off them.

"Her name is Cherry but it used to be Heather. There are some parts of her that seem older than me, but lots of new parts, too. It's a real pastiche."

I mix Alicia a drink while she retrieves a felt birthday hat for me, too, from her suitcase. Then she slices us both some lemon.

"But how did you get in?"

She winces. "I broke your bathroom window. By mistake. I went to give it a little jiggle, to see if it was unlocked, and I didn't think it would really shatter but it totally did."

"Shatter?"

"But guess what I'm getting you for your birthday? A new window! And . . ."

"Let me guess. You?"

"Me!"

We clink glasses and then, like every year, we recount our favorite birthdays together—all of them in Santa Fe when we were young and broke and catering other people's extravagant parties.

Near the bottom of her cocktail she says, "I really am so sorry about the window."

I shrug, letting her know not to worry about it. "Oliver can replace it. He's a full-on Property Brother now, remember?"

The vodka is making me floaty and warm. Or maybe it's being with Alicia.

She rests her head on my shoulder. "Tell me everything. How was therapy? I need to know, like, from the minute you walked into Miriam's. I was telling the woman next to me on the plane—you would love her, a retired nurse from Savannah and a massive Louise Penny fan; dead ringer for Heidi Klum's mom, or what I imagine her mom looks like—anyway, I told her all about how you and Oliver were going to tell your therapist that you were finally ready to be handcuffed and she's dying to know what happens next. So I do have to text her later. But first, I'm starving."

For dinner we find a BBQ restaurant with sawdust on the floor and bottomless soda refills.

"*Vogue?* This is the best!" Alicia grins over an ear of corn.

"Everyone will know that I'm Dirty Diana."

"Finally! I am so ready."

"I'm glad you are?"

"Diana, what's the worst that can happen? Detractors—mostly anonymous and online—will call you a slut? Depraved. Sex-obsessed. Selfish and unlikable? Because why? You're advocating for pleasure?"

"That's depressing."

"More depressing, some of the hate will come from other women because we've been told it's impolite to ask for what we want. We've been conditioned to take less money, less power . . . less say over our own bodies. We've been told to please our man so many times we've forgotten that we can experience pleasure, too."

"So I should be excited about the *Vogue* piece?" I grin.

"You'll also be celebrated. Because you are starting a conversation so many women have been dying to have."

After less than an hour in Alicia's presence, the stress of going public gradually melts away as we catch up on our lives. After dinner, she flags down a waiter and he brings us a warm blueberry cobbler. Alicia grins but it quickly falters—an expression, faraway and sad, crosses her face. Then she smiles again and grabs her purse to find a box of rainbow-colored candles. She sticks one in our dessert and lights it. "Make a wish?"

I close my eyes and imagine a world where I've already told Oliver about the site and we feel as close as we did the day Emmy was born. Then I blow the candle out. When I open them again, Alicia's own eyes are shiny with tears. "What's wrong?"

"Nothing." She shakes her head. "Something. I don't know."

"Is it Nico?"

"I'm just tired. Mom-tired. I probably need to get my hormones checked. I'm sure some testosterone would perk me right up."

"What is it?"

She picks at the cobbler with her fork then sighs and pushes it away. "I don't know. It's been fun watching you get back to painting and building the site. You're making stuff. Like we always said we would. All I'm making these days is beige food. That's literally all Elvis will eat. French fries and banana pancakes. But it's not just that. If you told me while I was in grad school that I'd be teaching film instead of making my own films, I wouldn't have believed you. I had so much confidence to just *do*. I don't know where that went."

"You haven't been sitting around doing nothing. Look how much you've helped me this year. And your students. They love you."

"Meh. Let's face it, they don't really deserve my wisdom." She grins then, trying to tell me not to worry. "And I can't get that saying out of my head. The one that haunts every teacher. Those who can . . ."

"Oh, please."

"I know. But. It's like time sped up. I thought I had so much of it. Then I woke up old. And people who hire directors don't want old."

"You thought we were old when we were in our twenties. Remember?"

"But now we might really be. Old."

"There is always an appetite for creative and brilliant female directors with strong visions."

A woman across the room laughs—a little raspy and a little too loud—and the sound is so familiar that we both snap our heads in her direction expecting to see L'Wren. But the woman who laughed is a total stranger to us both.

"I wish she were here," Alicia says.

"Me too."

"You still haven't spoken?"

"We've spoken. We've even seen each other around school. But it's different."

"What do you think she would say? If she were here now?"

"To you?"

Alicia nods.

"I think she would say . . . 'listen to your heart.'"

Alicia nearly chokes on her Dr Pepper. "She definitely would not."

"Fine. You're right. She'd say, 'Direct a cat movie and I'll write the check.'"

Alicia's expression softens. I reach for her hand across the table. "Elvis is still little," I say. "He's barely in school full-time. And the lie that you can do it all, all at once . . . it's not just untrue, it's mean. There's a whole part of your brain still recovering from the soup of having a baby."

"I know." Her bottom lip quivers.

"And you're about to find the next great thing you're excited about making. And it's going to be brilliant."

"Ugh. Nico really does owe you a thank-you." She wipes her tears with a BBQ wet nap. "And while we're crying into our barbecue and this couple is pretending not to eavesdrop"—Alicia tilts her head toward the next table and neither of its occupants bothers to look away—"can I just say, you're doing the right thing, Diana. With Oliver. Date your husband."

"But I want to have sex with my husband."

"Date your husband so you can eventually fuck your husband."

"Mmm." I finish my soda. "Miriam would like you so much."

"Right? God, I do really love winning a therapist's approval. Probably why therapy never works so great for me. You really are doing the right thing. Oh, that reminds me." She composes a text to her new airplane friend, reciting loud enough for the next table to hear. "Therapist told them to date. No crotchless panties. Yet. More later." She hits send. "I think it's hot. Like a tantric marriage or something. Can you imagine what's going to happen when you finally have sex?"

"Tantric? You think we'll go for hours?"

Alicia snorts. "No. God no. Oliver's gonna come in like negative two seconds."

That night I sleep with my bedroom door open so I can hear Alicia's light snoring from the guest room. I lie awake feeling grateful for the familiar, reassuring sound in this otherwise empty house. I try to make a plan to help Alicia, something that will get her to stumble into the next thing. I tell myself to fall asleep and maybe it'll come to me in a dream. But at 12:30 I'm still wide awake with no plan. On the nightstand, my phone buzzes.

A text from Oliver:

> You missed a mean eggs Benedict at my mom's.
> AND SO MANY OBJECTIONABLE COMMENTS.

I laugh to the empty room and type:

> Remember the time your cousin brought his vegetarian girlfriend and your dad just lied and said the ham was vegan?

> That was a bold move. For both of them.

> I do miss your mom's meringue pie...

> That she pretended to bake herself?

> ???!!! I'm sorry... what?

> From a bakery in McKinney.

No wonder she would never give me the recipe.

> I brought you a slice. Sending it home tomorrow with Emmy.

Thank you.

There is a pause. Three lingering dots, and then he finally adds:

I'm lying here planning our first date.

> Very exciting.

I'm having a hard time. Ok to admit that?

> Of course.

I googled "where to take your wife who is still your wife but you might be getting back together with depending on how dating goes."

> What'd Siri have to say?

Chick-fil-A

> Nice.

She pinned every location within 30 miles.

> I do love waffle fries.

Nope. Still not sexy. I'm going to come up with something great.

> It doesn't have to be sexy.

Fine. Chick-fil-A it is.

                              Can't wait.

Really?

                              Really.

You know what's really great about dating your wife? You don't have to play it cool and pretend you're not excited.

Chapter Three

I don't know what to expect. A combination of dinner and . . . something. Maybe dinner and a movie. A walk and a coffee? As long as it's not a bowling alley or an ice-skating rink, I'll be fine. Something about being surrounded by other couples on a first date as we're starting over makes me too self-conscious.

We begin the night at Keller's Drive-In, an old-fashioned diner and one of our favorite spots when we were first dating. I loved it back then because I could afford to treat even though I was broke. It's raining again, so we eat in Oliver's truck with the windows rolled up, and the conversation is easy. I ask him about work and he tells me about the house he recently flipped. We finish our burgers and I find myself not wanting the date to end despite the rain now coming down in heavy sheets. It's strange, sitting next to Oliver and wishing, greedily hoping, for more and more time. Like the feeling of finally being in the warm glow of a secret crush.

After dinner, he surprises me and we drive another ten minutes to an interactive museum he read about. I can't remember the last time we've been to a museum together. Maybe when Emmy was an infant? When weekends went on forever and we craved anywhere we could walk in air-conditioned loops while she napped in her stroller.

The entrance to the museum is through a giant, glittering mall. Easter decorations are everywhere, with Mother's Day nipping at its heels.

Inside, the museum is like a gigantic set made to look like a family home, all under one roof, the way I imagine an enormous, old-Hollywood soundstage would be. Oliver leads us into what looks like a real foyer but is an interactive space with mail to read and phones to scroll through. There is a stack of headphones on the dining room table so we each take a pair and hit play. At first, there's only music, an eerie fairy-tale soundtrack. Then a woman's voice, soft and lilting, tells us that a mystery lies within the exhibit and we are encouraged to find clues. We're surrounded by visitors who look like they've been here for hours combing for clues about what happened to the precocious young boy who went missing after discovering an otherworldly creature. There are missing posters with his picture on the coffee table and home movies of the family, even a phone with old text messages you can take turns dissecting for leads. By the third room, my mind is spinning in directions as odd as the soft-voiced narrative.

My attention wanders from the task in front of us and instead I begin to imagine what a museum of my own marriage to Oliver would look like. What would happen if we let fifty strangers wander our house to investigate when and where we went wrong? What, exactly, was lost and when? What if they picked through our mail or scrolled through years of our text messages? The beginnings: can't stop thinking about you. The middle: make sure you buy the kind of bread Emmy likes for her lunch and Have you seen the remote? It's not in the couch. And finally: I'll be home late. Don't wait up.

Would those be the relevant clues? Or would it be the lack of art on the walls because we could never agree on what should be hung where? Or the couch pillows in the living room misshapen from Oliver sleeping downstairs so often? The temperature that was never quite right? Too cold for me, too hot for Oliver. Or would it be less of a physical clue and more of a feeling?

I follow Oliver through the narrow halls of the exhibit. I'm flooded with the sudden need to find this boy.

I pull off my headphones and Oliver does the same. "What are we missing?"

"It looks complicated," he says. "Maybe more fun just to observe?"

"Excuse me?" I find a staffer with the most beautiful blue hair and brown eyes, wearing fairy wings and a cowboy hat. "Do most people find the missing boy?"

"Mostly. There are clues everywhere."

"So that's the game? That's how we win?"

She looks confused by my question, the competitive edge in my voice, but then she grins and says, "Pay close attention to the electronics."

We find the family computer and watch home videos of the missing boy talk about new discoveries and a monster that he believes lives in his house. When this doesn't help, Oliver suggests, "We haven't read all the postcards yet?"

We relax into the cozy guest room and sit down on the bed. It's just us in here for now and the fake window is open and there's a fan blowing to simulate a breeze. Oliver smells fresh and clean, and I have the sudden urge to kiss the nape of his neck. I scoot closer into him, pretending it's to get a better look at the postcards but really I just want to be near him. I picture us in a long slow kiss. We could lean back into this bed and stay here until the museum closes.

Oliver smiles, reading my mind. "Don't you want to find him?"

I take in all the clues in this room: the clocks all stopped at 7:06 P.M., the purposefully rumpled blankets on the floor, the tap from the bathroom set to a steady drip. All around us, museumgoers come and go, a swarm of serious-looking treasure hunters and Keith Morrison obsessives.

Oliver shifts beside me on the bed. His knee grazes mine and a shiver runs through me. We'll never be able to solve the mystery. Our brains are too fuzzy. They can only handle one strong urge at a time, and my desire to be close to Oliver is all I can focus on. With my lips to his ear, I whisper, "Let's go."

"Go where?"

"Somewhere. Just you and me."

When Oliver stands, I can see the outline of his erection, tight against his jeans. It makes me feel giddy and ridiculous and powerful all at once. I smile and follow him through the haunted backyard like we're moving through a dream. Our desire for each other is floating us through this dark space on a cloud.

And then it hits me, all at once. Under the faux stars of this unfamiliar backyard, like a slap in the face, I realize exactly how strangers would know we were doomed.

It would be Oliver's dirty socks in our laundry basket.

At some point, I had stopped washing them. A quiet protest to the inescapable panic that I had become his mother, maybe. Or that we no longer saw all the million little things we did for each other. There was a tally being taken and we both, silently, dug in. Our domestic tasks remained split down the middle, and I didn't stop doing laundry altogether, but something in me refused to wash another pair of his socks. And he didn't bend either. He was equally good at this game, carrying equal parts resentment. He started wearing my socks, which horrified me. Then a pair of fuzzy snowmen Christmas socks from his mother, then trampoline socks from the local bounce house. I stopped washing his socks and he stopped bringing me cold water for my nightstand. First we gave up on the little things and then flat out begrudged the others.

The realization leaves me feeling cold, then slightly panicked, like we've overstayed our welcome in a place we were already unwelcome. I rush us through the rest of the exhibit to the exit. Let the boy stay missing. It's really none of our business.

We're spit out of the exhibit's exit into the mall's atrium. I follow Oliver's gaze to the Claire's Accessories that Emmy would have spotted and then begged us to have her ears pierced. "Should we have brought her?"

I look up into Oliver's blue-green eyes, bright and calm. He takes my hand and I feel the familiar reassurance of his touch. The panicked feeling washes away, followed by a charge, a headiness as he closes the space between us. I make a sound, a muffled giggle that I quickly swallow.

"What is it?"

I press my lips together and shake my head thinking of those two faraway souls and their dirty socks. Far enough away that it's like a funny story. Inconvenient details of a stranger's life. A house full of them. "Nothing. I'm just happy."

Oliver lifts my chin. I slip my arms around his neck and pull him close. We kiss like this for a long time, under the bright lights of the mall at night.

On our second date, Oliver and I drive to a dance hall in Mesquite. He always surprises me on the dance floor. He shouldn't be this good at it. He played baseball and was in the chess club. He wore pressed khakis as a teenager and tucked in his polo shirts.

But the first time he led me onto a dance floor he moved so effortlessly. Never too showy or too drunk, just comfortable in his own body, the easiest dance partner from one song to the next. I liked that no one ever seemed to notice this the same way I did, like only I could really see him and, therefore, he was all mine.

The tin-ceilinged dance hall is dressed up in strands of white lights. Inside it's cavernous and wood-beamed with a bar near the front where you don't dare ask for anything fancier than a Jack and Coke. It's loud and happy and people are here to dance. Oliver leads me onto the dance floor, down in front near the stage, and takes my hand in his, warm and strong.

I once asked him where he learned to dance so well and he had shrugged. "Cotillion. Where every hormonal Texas teen with sweaty palms learns how."

I ask him again tonight and he gives me a similar shrug.

"Really, where'd you learn to two-step? Not at cotillion."

"No, it was with my great-grandmother Ruby. Her nursing home had dances the first Friday of every month and I was her preferred partner. I was at the peak of my awkward preteen years, when only your grandma would be proud to have you on her arm."

"I bet you were very cute together."

"She was fun. Always hatching a plan for what to do next. And she had no patience for most people and zero interest in small talk, especially over the phone. If anyone called—and it could be the Queen—she would say, 'Hello. So nice to talk, and thank you for calling.' And then hang up. That was it."

"I really like her now." How could we be together so long and still have new stories to share? I feel the warm bloom of optimism in my chest.

"She would have liked you too."

Oliver takes confident steps forward as I step back—quick-quick-slow—then he pulls me close and studies me for a beat, as if suddenly deciding I'm a safe space.

"Ruby's first husband, Earl, died on an oil rig and left her all his money. She married my great-grandfather, but I don't think she ever got over Earl."

Familiar sensations of our early courtship come rushing back to me. Oliver's easy smile. The feel of his strong hands on my back. The assured way he leads me across the dance floor. I'm free-falling off a cliff and he's there to catch me. He spins me away from him and then quickly back in, scooping me up and into his body, so close almost a kiss.

"To Earl."

"To Earl." Oliver smiles and I beam. I love that I can still make him happy. That his eyes light up when he looks at me. That might have been the worst part of our breakup—the fact that for months we couldn't hold each other's gaze.

A man in a well-worn Stetson approaches us, moving slowly and deliberately. His eyes are a milky blue and his dark, pressed Wranglers hang from his frame.

"May I?" he interrupts, a soggy toothpick dancing in the corner of his mouth. "We don't get women this pretty in here often." His voice is gravelly and warm.

Over his shoulder a woman in a peach-colored dress, who I assume is his wife, smiles at me, relieved, I can tell, to sit this one out. "Of course."

As we dance, I notice Oliver watching, leaning against the wall and sipping his beer. His eyes never leave me. The dance hall swirls as my surprisingly spritely dance partner spins me around. Oliver appears in brief flashes before me, like passing someone on a merry-go-round. With every revolution, I want him more.

As the song ends, Oliver nears and waits for the music to slow. "I think your wife might be getting jealous."

My partner claps Oliver on the shoulder. "I'd tell her to go to hell but she's headed there anyway." He winks at us and does a swivel of his hips as he walks toward her.

As we watch him go, Oliver asks, "I could never, right?"

"What? Say something like that and still be mildly charming." I turn my body to face his. "No, never."

Oliver chuckles. He takes me in his arms and pulls me close. I feel the warmth of his body. My breasts pressed against his chest. His arms are stronger now from working outside of an office. His blue-green eyes dazzle. He's my husband, but he's new.

Please let this last. This feeling. We keep dancing, both of us willing ourselves to stay in the moment. Let another Willie Nelson cover song comfort us as I follow Oliver's lead. We dance as if we've danced together our whole lives and never stopped. *Blue eyes crying in the rain.*

The ride home is thick with anticipation. I shift in my seat, restless, wanting to be reckless and break all the rules. I think of reaching for his knee, sliding my hand up his thigh. I picture his surprise. The sharp intake of breath. The delight as he pulls the car over and I climb into his lap.

Take it slow. Date.

I clasp my hands together and turn to watch the familiar blur of our neighborhood out my window.

When we arrive at the house, he parks in the driveway and walks me to our door. We linger too long.

"Do you want to come in?"

"I'm not sure I've ever wanted anything more."

I smile as I fish for my keys. "So come in. We don't have to tell Miriam."

We're close now, our chests nearly touching, and I know his heart is beating as fast as mine. Desire doesn't politely bloom in our bodies, it thunders, demanding attention. I stand on my tiptoes, my lips gently brushing against his. "Come in," I whisper into his mouth.

He leans in a fraction, then exhales, his body shuddering against mine. "I want to. I want to spend the whole night together."

"Me too."

"We can't mess this up, Diana. Now that I have you again, I don't want to make a single wrong move." He rocks back on his heels and just that little bit of space he creates between us is like an ice-cold bath.

My senses sharpen. I notice the yellow glow of the light above Oliver, the annoying way it creates an angelic halo around his head, and hear the sound of a moth circling the bulb. I sigh. "Neither do I."

I stay in the doorway and watch him drive away. My tears make his red taillights blur until finally I can't see his car at all. Inside, the house is quiet. I run a bath and think about how badly I wanted him to stay. But it feels different from the way I wanted him to stay when he was moving out. I was so afraid of what it would feel like to be in this house without him—too empty, too quiet, too lonely. It hadn't lost that feeling, even after so many months. But tonight, the desire for him to stay is different. It's not the safety of him that I crave. I want him to stay with every ounce of my being. I want to feel his naked skin against mine and wake up to more of him in the morning. I crave him. His body. Our sex.

> *In my fantasy, I'm back in college taking a final that I've been studying for all month. I'm more than prepared. I ace the test. I answer every question confidently and quickly. We still have twenty minutes left but I've checked my answers twice and I know I've gotten them all correct. With five minutes remaining, my professor reminds us to complete the backside of the test as well. Horrified, I turn the test over and see fifty complex word problems without solutions and I'm so panicked I have a powerful orgasm. Something about running out of time always does it for me. As the time whittles away and I race to finish, the orgasms come fast and furious.*

Chapter Four

For the first time in weeks, on a chilly April day, it finally stops raining for more than a few hours and L'Wren invites me to play tennis. We've seen each other at school drop-off and at our girls' playdates, but it has always felt forced. We were like two stressed newscasters during a technical difficulty.

That night last fall, when I told L'Wren about Dirty Diana, she was rightfully upset. I had kept it from her for months, scared she would distance herself from me if she knew. But she ended up distancing herself because she *didn't* know. Because I didn't give her a chance to be close.

I'm first at the courts and I stand next to my car, hopping lightly from one foot to the other to stay warm until L'Wren arrives.

She pulls up moments later and pops open her trunk, grabs her racquet, and hands me two new cans of balls. "Look at me, out on the public courts!" Her smile is wide and sunny but it's partly performance. There is a hesitancy in her quick embrace.

As we head toward the courts she drops her chin and whispers, "These folks are like vultures, Diana. I had to sign up weeks ago for this slot—and now look, I can see them circling."

We open the chain-link fence gate and I scan the courts for vultures but there is only an innocent-looking couple, thin and elderly, lobbing gentle shots across the net.

"Thanks for inviting me," I say. We take our place on court #2 and hang our bags on the bench.

"Kevin kept the club membership in the divorce."

"Can't you both belong?"

"Ugh, and run into him there on dates?" She pulls her foot to her hamstring, stretching her long, lean legs. "See him at the bar, surrounded by admirers? You've always assumed my ego is healthier than it is." She's still tan from her recent trip to Turks and Caicos. I only know where she's been because of what her stepson, Liam, has told me. "The truth is, this is a great court. Who needs the club?"

Behind us, the chain-link fence creaks open and two men stroll onto our court, as if we aren't even here—one tall with long hairy legs and short shorts, and the other in a snug-fitted windbreaker.

L'Wren pulls her arm across her chest, still stretching. "This court is reserved."

"But you're not even playing," the taller one protests.

The shorter one points his racquet in my direction. "And that one is wearing black-soled shoes! She shouldn't even be on the court!"

"We're preparing, a-holes," L'Wren snaps. And when they freeze in surprise she adds, "No one kicks my best friend off a public court! Shoo!"

She turns and winks at me. And then the two of us are cracking up, and some of the tension gives way.

She fixes the misfolded corner of my collared shirt. "I missed you."

"I missed you too."

L'Wren smiles and jogs to the baseline. We take some warm-up shots—easy hits down the middle.

She returns my first serve, calling, "Do you think I'm a prude?"

"No," I shout across the net.

"I can talk about sex."

"I know."

"Then why? Why did you keep everything so secret?"

"I think . . . I was afraid of letting you down."

"What's that?"

"I didn't want to let you down!" I shout.

Instead of swinging her racquet, L'Wren catches the ball in her palm. "How would that let me down?"

I join her at the net. "Because you'd feel obligated to protect me. And I'm going to need your protection again."

"I'll always protect you. We're friends, Diana."

"But I don't want you to have to. That shouldn't be your job. I want to protect you sometimes."

"You will." She pushes down on the net and, with her long legs, climbs over it. She pulls me into a hug.

"I won't," I argue. "You're too strong." I can smell her jasmine perfume and feel the familiar edges of her bony shoulders.

"Ha. I'm a mess," she whispers into my hair.

"You're so not a mess."

We volley back and forth for the next half hour and it feels good not thinking about anything else but returning her shot.

The weather is temperate and the court shaded, but we're dripping with sweat as we break for water. Still breathing hard, L'Wren confesses, "I selfishly loved that you were getting a divorce so I would have someone to be divorce partners with."

"Isn't Arthur technically your divorce partner?"

Since splitting with Kevin, L'Wren has been dating her perfect match—Arthur is a very handsome vet who shares her love of rescuing every creature, the homelier the better to love.

"He's been a divorce gem. Seriously. He's made it too easy."

"See? You don't need me for that."

"No, I still want you to be getting a divorce. But it's okay if you aren't. Are you?"

"I'm dating." Before she can get too excited I add, "Oliver. We're dating each other."

L'Wren goes quiet. I fight the urge to ramble on and convince her why this is a good thing.

"I'm happy for you, Diana. I really am. And I love Oliver."

"But?"

"Well, you're right, I am protective of you. I know what it's like to be married to someone and grow apart from each other. I don't know how you get back there. Is that a thing? I mean, I know couples get back together, but I always assumed it was out of necessity. Like they forced the marriage for their kids or it was a financial decision or they just weren't happy on their own. But when you and Oliver broke up and we were in Paris, you seemed *happier*. Whether you're with Jasper or not. Do you still talk to him? Jasper?"

"Not really. He's sent me a few photos, from wherever he's traveling, but it's all so polite when we text. A little sad. Like we're letting each other down gently, all over again, even though we're just saying hi. And now that Oliver and I are going to date . . . it's better not to be in touch with Jasper."

"So you're excited to date your husband?"

I nod.

"Truly?"

"Yes. And terrified, too, of course. What if we get back together and then six months from now, we slip right back into old patterns? What if we start to lose interest in each other again? What if I can't stand the way he chews an apple or my skin crawls when he asks me to send him an email reminder instead of writing it down himself. Or

I catch him studying his hairline obsessively in the mirror but pretending not to? Like something so small and ridiculous turns me off and I get weird about it and the thought of—"

"Okay, okay." L'Wren laughs. "As long as you're worrying enough for the both of us, I'll back off."

"I'm worried about it all. But I'm still excited."

"Good. I just need a tiny beat to catch up is all. Part of me is still back in Oliver-is-sleeping-with-Hat-Lady Land." She waves her hand to dismiss the dreary thought. "Can you believe Liam is getting married? That's what I've been dying to talk to you about."

"Sorry?" I must have misheard.

"He didn't tell you?"

"Married?"

"He told me and not you? Huh. I just assumed he would tell you first."

Me too. "He's engaged? To Kirby?"

"I say plan the wedding before she changes her mind. She's a real catch."

"So is Liam."

"For a certain person. Sure."

"L'Wren."

"Fine. He's a catch. We're all catches. Even Oliver." She grins but it quickly fades. "Diana? Does he know? About Dirty Diana."

"I've been trying to decide how to tell him."

"Don't. I mean do, eventually, but don't now. Let yourselves get back on track first. It will just complicate things."

"But I want to fall back in love with the version of Oliver that supports me in everything I do. That's a big part of this, isn't it? It can't be conditional."

"Of course, sure. But go on a few dates and see if there is still a *there* there. Then tell him."

"You don't think that's dishonest?"

"You've already been lying so what's a few more dates gonna do?"

"That's so sad."

She gives a playful sigh. "Sometimes we're sad now. It's who we are."

I'm hoping for a quiet Saturday at the Dirty Diana offices, but I arrive to a full house and a table full of vibrators of every shape and color. Over the past month, I've been greeted with everything from leather whips to upscale lingerie, each one a possible idea for a brand partnership.

Without looking up from the vibrators Petra chirps, "Vibezz—two z's—sent these." Then, "Trade you a vibrator for the *Vogue* questionnaire?"

She's flanked by two women I assume are new hires. The office space and staff seem to grow at every turn. I say hello and join them, hovering over the vibrators and arranging them in rainbow order, as if deep in decision-making, all so that I can avoid telling her the questionnaire is buried deep in my email inbox, untouched.

"Lynnie and Max are helping with social. They'll float over some posts later for your approval. The micro-fantasies are getting lots of love. Maybe a haiku fantasy is next? Short content is working nicely."

"Why not one word?" Kirby jokes, joining us at the table.

"'Hot'?" Now Liam is here and it's an entire team meeting around a table of vibrators. I know I shouldn't care, but being near Liam reminds me of the sting of his unshared news. I catch myself glancing at Kirby's ring finger—of course, there's an engagement ring—and I feel worse. How did I miss it?

"We're partial to the purple one," Liam offers. "It really did the trick. Right, Kirby?"

"Really?" It comes out sharper than I meant. "You're telling your co-workers?" I catch a flash of hurt in Liam's eyes. I've managed to embarrass him in front of everyone.

"Uh. We're not exactly selling bibles here?" He gestures around the office space. "So . . . yeah?"

"It doesn't bother me," Kirby chimes in, but her cheeks have gone bright pink with embarrassment. "Why should it?"

Petra changes the subject. "I think the Dirty Diana brand should go for a solo vibrator. You can listen to our fantasies and do what you like in the privacy of your own bedroom. You don't need a partner to listen."

"I kind of like the idea of a Dirty Diana vibrator for couples," I counter. "Couples that are new or couples that are reconnecting . . ."

Petra chuckles. "*We get it.* You're back with Oliver."

"We are not. Not really. It's not just about Oliver. It's about our story. A backward love story."

"What does that have to do with Dirty Diana and vibrators?"

"I'm Diana. So." I blush a deep pink.

At lunchtime, I knock on Liam's open door, but he doesn't hear with his headphones on. Or at least, pretends not to hear. Inside, it's dimly lit but surprisingly tidy. The only mess is a torn-open bag of Razzles spilled across his desk. He tosses out the yellow ones and snacks on the rest as he types.

I knock again, and this time he looks up. He pulls off his headphones, his hair a mess of curls in every direction. I take this as an invitation to enter.

"I have to head out soon so this is your only chance to get me to Panchos. I promise to stop talking about the hair we found in our salsa last time. We leave in ten seconds or we never go again."

Liam barely cracks a smile but grabs his keys. At least for the moment, he's counting my burrito offer as a satisfactory apology.

"Let me talk about it in a way you can understand." Only Liam can both mansplain to me and charm me at the same time. Before our food has even arrived, he is once again pitching me on why we should try creating a Dirty Diana fantasy on film. "For example, say Lululemon puts out a special legging. . . ."

"Is that what you think I am? A Lululemon mom?"

"You're wearing Lululemon right now."

"These are L'Wren's. I wear her hand-me-downs."

"No offense, D. But own it."

"They do last forever . . ."

"Okay. Fine. Different example. Tiny's Milk & Cookies. What Texan doesn't love Tiny's? You would think they would have a lot of different types of cookies, right? They don't. They stick to what they know."

"Exactly my point," I say.

"Hang on. They're famous for their chocolate chip but they also have coffee. And ice cream. Pastries. But they're known for their cookie."

"My point again. What am I missing?"

"They can't survive on the chocolate chip cookies alone," Liam says. "So they just introduced their ginger cookie after years of development. And that shit has been sold out for months. I can't even get one."

"Neither can I."

"The ginger cookie is video. The coffee is your paintings. The ice cream is the vibrator collab. When sharks stop swimming, they die. We have to continue to expand."

"Sharks? That's your metaphor?"

"If you want to keep growing . . ."

"We are growing. Our fans love the fantasies."

"And for a while, the chocolate chip cookie was enough for Tiny's."

"I'll think about it."

"Will you?"

"I promise." He studies my expression until he's satisfied I'm telling the truth.

"Good. Now lay it on me." He takes a sip of his water. "I know I'm in trouble."

"Why didn't you tell me?"

He doesn't pretend not to know what I'm talking about. He would never do that to me. "Right after I proposed—and after I got over the shock that Kirby actually said yes—part of me thought it would be better for you, and for L'Wren, if I told her first. Your friendship has been on kind of weird, shaky ground and I thought maybe if she had a secret this time around, something you had no idea about, she might feel kind of powerful and, I don't know, more forgiving of you?"

"Oh." Our server sets down our iced tea and I take a long, cold sip. "Dammit. That is a good reason. Perceptive." I narrow my eyes at him, trying to decide if he's being completely honest. "Too perceptive?"

He holds my gaze and then breaks into a grin, his mirth blossoming. "It worked, right? You two are right as rain again."

"L'Wren called you already?"

"She texted me to say thank you. Inviting you to tennis may have been my idea."

"Oh. Well, thank you. But . . ." I smooth the napkin in my lap. "I get the sense you didn't want to tell me at all."

Liam exhales, long and slow, blows the perfect brown curls from his forehead. "I guess that's the other part. Telling L'Wren I was engaged was easy. I know how much she likes Kirby. I'm marrying up and L'Wren would be the first to think it. But you . . ."

"I like Kirby too."

"I know."

"I would have been happy for you. I am happy for you."

"But . . ."

"But nothing. I would have had a perfectly normal reaction to your news."

"Uh-huh." He nods slowly, as if to say *go on* so I do.

"A perfectly normal reaction, which probably for normal people would include some bit of concern."

"See? This is what I was trying to avoid."

"Liam. You haven't been dating that long. You're both so young. You've never even lived on your own." He flinches like I've pinched him. "Sometimes it's hard to be sure with all that working against you."

Our food arrives and Liam dives into his burrito. He swallows a big bite before he says, "I am sure. I wouldn't have asked her if I wasn't sure."

"Of course. I just mean, look at my own wobbly, house-of-cards relationship with Oliver. Even when you think you know someone, you might not really know someone."

"Kirby and I don't keep secrets from each other."

This time I flinch. "Fine. Maybe not secrets. But you don't know how she's going to react in important situations. Time is really all that can tell you that. Time around each other. In every situation. Like what if you pass a car accident and she doesn't want to slow down to help because you're late for something or—"

"I should have waited for us to stumble onto a car wreck before I proposed?"

Liam's defensiveness only makes me dig in harder. "No, Liam. But you haven't even lived with each other yet."

"I'm in love."

"And that's not necessarily enough."

"When did you become so anti-romantic?"

"I don't know?" I pick at the bored and wilted salad on my plate. "It just happens?"

"I really like you, Diana. Obviously. And I don't mean to be an asshole"—here it comes and I deserve it—"but Kirby and I are nothing like you and Oliver."

Even though I braced myself, the punch still lands. "I didn't say you were."

"We trust each other. We've trauma-dumped. Like a lot. She knows all about my shitty relationship with my mom and I know all about her anxiety and everything she's afraid of, like Pomeranians and the sound of a dishwasher at night in an empty house." He speaks faster now, emphatically, without taking a breath, "And honestly, deep down, if I picture driving by a car wreck with her, I don't give a fuck whether or not she stops to help. Or even slows down. Because really, as long as she calls 911, I think we're good." He takes a stab at his burrito with a fork. "And I do believe she would call 911. Okay?"

Chapter Five

"Where did you go? When you were out of touch for that long weekend last year?"

May has almost arrived and Oliver and I drift in a canoe in the middle of a crystal blue lake.

"Fourth of July? You know where I was." We've paddled far from the shore and now we're lying on our backs, our heads at opposite ends of the canoe. It isn't a large boat, so our feet reach the other person's hip.

"I don't know. Not really."

"I was with someone."

"Jasper?"

He can't see me nod, but he already knows the answer.

"What kind of name is that?"

"Oliver."

"Sorry. It's a fine name. If we'd had a son, I absolutely would have named him Jasper."

I give his hip a gentle shove with my foot.

"Seriously, tell me about him."

"Why?" I prop myself onto my forearms so I can read his expression, which is gentle and genuine.

"I'm curious. I don't know him at all."

"He was an old friend." I lie back down. "From New Mexico."

"You dated him back then?"

"Yes."

"Why did you break up?"

I hesitate. How much does he want to know? I was in love with Jasper and when he left Santa Fe I was heartbroken.

"He wasn't ready to commit," I say.

"But you wanted to. Commit."

"I thought I did. The truth is, it was easy for me to be so sure because I always kind of knew he wasn't ready. So there was no reason for me to worry about the commitment."

"So he broke up with you?"

Above us, the sky is turning from orange to a purple gray, and I worry it'll grow dark faster than we think. "Yeah. He broke up with me. In a vague kind of way that only Jasper can manage."

"Were you upset?"

"Devastated. But I was young and I had never been in love before. It was before I met you."

"Did you ever think about him? After we married?"

All the time. Especially during the last few years. Sometimes I would imagine it was Jasper I was making love to.

"Why are you asking me all this?"

"I want to know. He seems like he was a big part of your life and you never told me about him."

"What about the women you dated?"

"What about them? I'll tell you anything."

"Do you still think about any of them?"

"No."

"Not even Katherine?"

"Sometimes. But not in the way you're thinking."

"Why not?"

"I think of other things. She was kind. And funny. And there was an ease to her."

"New relationships are always easy." I can't help it. "Sorry. I asked. Go on."

"Emmy and Taylor got along, so it was easy for all of us to be together. Some of the women I dated when you and I first separated were younger and didn't have kids so they liked to go out a lot. I didn't have to stay up all night with Katherine. We could do things like order pizza and take it to the park."

"I get it." I try to find shapes in the clouds so I don't have to picture their picnics in the park.

"And I liked her body."

"Oh." A sensation takes me by surprise—not jealousy, maybe, but longing. My own body comes alive. Pays attention.

"What about her body?"

Oliver sits up and begins to paddle. I think he's trying to change the subject until I realize he's rowing us to a more secluded part of the lake.

"Why aren't you answering?"

"Do you really want to know?"

"I do. I want to know."

As the words leave my lips a reckless charge runs through us both. We're both sitting at attention, facing each other.

"She had a nice ass. She did this thing where she would wrap her legs around me when we had sex. I liked that."

My pulse quickens. "What else?"

"I could make her come. And she was really loud when she came.

She didn't care. Even when she would talk dirty. It was . . . unexpected. And I realized how much I liked it."

"What did she say? When she spoke dirty?"

"Come on, Diana. Why are we talking about this?" The smile in his voice tells me he's enjoying this as much as I am.

"I just want to know. I told you about Jasper."

"She'd say, 'spread me open.' She'd tell me she needed me inside her."

I feel a warmth between my legs, and my breath catches in my throat. "How did you make her come?"

Oliver tilts his head up to the sky, as if trying to remember all the various ways. "She would kind of melt into me. And let me try things."

"Like what?"

"Different positions. She liked anal sex."

"Really?"

"I liked it too."

He watches for my reaction. Our knees our touching now, and I want so badly to reach for him.

"Jasper knew exactly how to make me orgasm."

Oliver swallows. His casualness is forced. I don't have to look to know he's growing hard. "He did?"

"Yes."

"How?"

Do I tell him all the ways? His fingers, his mouth, his words . . .

"It was a position. A certain position."

"Which one?" Oliver rests his fingers on my thigh, just below the drape of my skirt. A shiver runs through my body.

"When I was on top. Or on my side while he was touching me."

"Where did he touch you?"

I keep my eyes locked on his as I pull my skirt up my leg, higher and higher. Then I let my legs fall open, showing him my white cotton underwear. "Here." I touch myself over the fabric.

"Do you still think about him?"

"Not in a way that should worry you."

"Did you love him?" He hasn't taken his eyes off mine.

"Yes. At different times in my life."

Oliver smiles, warm and playful. He takes us over the cliff with his grin. He leans into me and places his hand over mine, between my legs.

My heart pounds. I want Oliver to keep touching me, to press harder, to rub his fingers against me. "Do you still think about Katherine?"

"Sometimes. She wanted me so badly. It felt good. It made me feel good."

I like the idea of another woman desiring my husband. Like he's a celebrity, universally adored by women. I let the fantasy wash over me, looking up at the darkening sky, from our nowhere place in the middle of the lake. With Oliver, sweet, handsome, and deceptively strong. He looks like a 1950s movie star. A beach-blanket, dazzling boyfriend of Gidget's, with sparkling green eyes, rosy lips, and a perfect smile. I throw my head back and bite my lip in anticipation of more—more of his touch, the feeling of him inside me. *What's your fantasy?* I close my eyes and I imagine Oliver striding out of the ocean with a surfboard under one arm and taking his cheery, bikinied girlfriend under a towel and fucking her from behind on the sand.

He pulls his hand away. "I couldn't get enough."

I open my eyes, but he won't meet my gaze. "Couldn't get enough of what?" I ask.

"You know."

"Show me."

"Diana." He tries to warn me, but his breathing is jagged.

"We don't have to touch . . . Just show me."

Oliver slowly unzips his pants. His cock is so hard it nearly bursts through his boxers. "Diana . . ." He's lost in desire, his cheeks flushed with it. I can see how badly he wants to touch me. The canoe rocks gently, small waves lapping against it.

"It's okay," I whisper.

"What if someone sees us?"

But we're too far gone to care, both of us lightheaded with want.

"There's no one out here," I say. "It's just us."

"What would Miriam think?"

"I don't want to think about Miriam right now."

"I want to feel you again."

I slide closer until I'm in his lap, straddling his hips. The canoe rocks, and for a moment I freeze. I grab onto Oliver's shoulders and he steadies us both. We stay still. Perfectly still until the water calms again. I lift my hips slowly and lower them onto him. His erection presses against me. He runs his hand through my hair then pulls my face to his. As soon as his mouth touches mine, I want to devour him. His clean taste, his full lips, his muscular arms.

"I love you, Diana," he whispers. "It never went away. Even when I told you it had."

I wrap my arms around his neck and sit up straighter so that I can sink deeper into his lap, feeling him grow harder against the thin, wet fabric of my underwear. I want so badly to pull them aside so I can feel his skin against mine. But the temptation will be too great if we take off our clothes.

I kiss the base of his neck, then along his jaw. I gently tug on his earlobe with my teeth and whisper, "Remember the beginning, before we had sex . . ." Oliver smiles, remembering the times we made out for hours in his bedroom like teenagers. We move against each other now, harder and faster, feeling the heat of our bodies and never wanting to stop. The friction builds—of our clothes, of our skin—until nothing matters. Not getting caught. Not tipping over completely. Nothing matters but the heat between us. "Oliver," I moan and he kisses me, hard, our tongues moving in circles. Then he pulls away, my face in his hands. "Wait. We can't. Our first time can't happen in a canoe."

"Our first time?" It echoes across the lake and we both laugh—then quickly stop when we almost tip. We steady ourselves and lock eyes—us, a canoe, fully clothed, and scared to tip over—and we crack up all over again.

I'm at the Sydney Opera House watching La Traviata *next to a handsome stranger. We have our own Juliet balcony. I studied opera in college, by the way. I appreciate it. Honestly. And let's just say the bel canto makes me incredibly excited. So during a particularly hurried aria, I move toward the stranger's seat, pull up my black sparkling gown, and straddle him. The vocals flow through me as I slowly ride him and the coloratura scores our secret climax like it was written for us.*

Chapter Six

After an urgent text from the Parents League the night before—and after losing a coin toss with Oliver—I pick up L'Wren for a meeting at the home of Lorraine Duncan. To blatantly disregard an "emergency meeting" of the Parents League, held at the league president's home, is like sending a townwide memo that you'd prefer to homeschool after all.

We arrive at her Preston Hollow mansion at exactly nine A.M., each of us carrying a tray of freshly cut fruit. At the arched doorway, Lorraine's housekeeper takes our melon offering and ushers us through the great room and out into the backyard. The rolling green lawn is already filling with mothers and a sprinkling of fathers. To our right, several rows of folding chairs have been set out.

Beside me, L'Wren scans the crowd, larger than a typical Parents League meeting. She's usually so at ease in this crowd, but today

L'Wren is obviously tense. "I don't get it. Nothing on the WhatsApp chat. I don't like it. They better not sneak something on to the agenda like trying to kill my Spring Pet Adoption Fair. It took three years to get that approved."

"I'm sure they would have called you first."

L'Wren stops suddenly. "Hat Lady, three o'clock." I follow her gaze to Raleigh, a fellow school parent and the first woman Oliver dated after he moved out.

"You have to stop calling her that."

L'Wren shrugs. "Do we say hello?"

The last time I spoke to Raleigh we were arguing in the parking lot of Oliver's building. She knew about Dirty Diana and she was warning me—threatening me—about what might happen if Oliver found out about it. My mouth goes dry. "She seems busy." And she does, deep in conversation with a group of well-dressed fifth-grade moms.

"She's really worked her way back in," L'Wren observes. "Think she's still afraid of me?"

"Okay, easy. Let's get you a snack."

After a few pleasant hellos, we linger near the lavish spread of pastries and coffee. Our cut fruit has not made it onto the white-tableclothed buffet and L'Wren is back to worrying about why we're really here. "If there *are* any surprises, I hope it's just that someone is very ill. Or dying—"

"L'Wren!"

"What?" She presses a hand to her heart. "I mean someone really old, like Ms. Sheila, the music teacher? She's lived a wonderful life. Her husband passed last year. I'd love to plan a goodbye ceremony for her."

Our mutual friend Jenna bounds toward us, curls bouncing, vibrating with gossip to spill. She has made knowing everything that happens at school a full-time, unpaid job.

"I know why we're here," she says.

She pauses for effect until L'Wren rolls her eyes. "Jenna!"

"Remember Sarah Lamont? Rex's mom? Well, Rex's older sister, Harmony, is in fifth grade. Do you know Harmony? Tall girl, cute, plays lacrosse? Anyway, Sarah told me that apparently one of the fifth-grade girls"—Jenna stops to mouth *Aubrey*—"was giving lessons at the bike racks last Tuesday. On how to give a blow job."

"What?" L'Wren half laughs, half shouts.

"Right? Lorraine had a fit when she found out. Her daughter, Savannah, told her everything. You know Lorraine's the one who tried to get prayer back at chapel five days a week. Very into God."

"It's St. Mary's. Everyone is into God."

"But Lorraine is extra into God. She's blaming the whole thing on the sex ed class the fifth graders just had."

"That's ridiculous." I snort.

"Huh." L'Wren's eyes sweep the crowd. "So no one has died? Or is, like, seriously ill?"

"What? Died?" Jenna gives her a puzzled look. "Maybe Lorraine died a little that day." Jenna clutches her heart and pretends to faint against me. We hear a spoon clanking an iced-tea glass, and she hurries us to our seats. "Don't piss her off. Remember what Lorraine did to Adele?"

"Oh god," L'Wren moans. "That was awful."

"Who's Adele?" I ask.

"Exactly," Jenna says, meaningfully. Her eyes go big like her curls.

"Stop." I laugh. I squeeze into a folding chair between L'Wren and Jenna.

"I'm serious. Stay out of her way. Whatever happens today, I fully intend to clutch my pearls and play along."

I look to L'Wren for backup, but she only zips her fingers across her lips.

"Really? You too?"

She shrugs and whispers in my ear, "Not to be a complete a-hole, but you are already on unsteady ground here. Out of all of us, you especially need to stay quiet."

"What does that mean?" Jenna asks, instantly curious.

I shake my head just as Lorraine steps in front of us all.

Lorraine is nearly six feet tall, with perfect posture and coral lipstick that matches her coral nails. "Thank you, everyone, for being here on such short notice." When she clasps her hands together, her diamond rings sparkle. "I know we all have busy lives and busy schedules and busy kiddos. But as most of you know from our group chat . . ." She clears her throat as if to say, *Can I get through this? I will try. For all of you.* "On Tuesday, a group of our fifth-grade girls loitered at the bike racks and discussed oral sex and how to perform it. Giving explicit instructions to impressionable ears. I was horrified to hear that my own sweet daughter had received some of this information. Thank god Savannah and I are close enough that she knows she can tell her mama anything." A plane flies overhead and for a moment I'm distracted, wondering how much money Lorraine has spent trying to get the airport's flight path changed. How many letters has she written, how many meetings has she held, just like this one? "As most of you know I was very vocal about the sex ed curriculum this year. And now . . ." She stares with a look that says, *Ah well, a fait accompli you dummies could have avoided if you'd only listened to me.* "Now, parents, you know why. Our children deserve a chance to be children. This world wants them to grow up so fast. We can't protect them from everything, but the least we can do is send them to school in a safe space. A space where they can be children."

Everyone is silent and keeping very still. "I'm here today because I need all of us parents to rally and do right by our kiddos and get sex ed removed from the fifth-grade curriculum. Can I get everyone to raise a hand if you will support me in my petition to the administration?" Lorraine raises an arm awkwardly over her head.

One by one, hands go up. Even those on either side of me.

"L'Wren!"

"What? I can teach Halston what she needs to know myself. I'll get her a book and leave it open on the kitchen table like my mom did."

"This is so dumb," I whisper. "Sex ed is educational. It has nothing to do with robbing kids of their childhoods."

Lorraine silently counts the hands in the air.

L'Wren whispers back, "Diana. I'm telling you, if ever there was a moment to swim with the salmon, this is it. It's not worth the enemy."

"Wonderful!" Lorraine smiles, and hands return to laps. "But I see a few hands were not raised."

"Yikes . . ." Jenna murmurs.

"All right, I understand . . ." Lorraine smiles, but like a saltwater crocodile, all sharp teeth and ready to snatch. "This isn't a dictatorship, right, y'all? I can be fair. For those of you who do want this kind of sex talk as part of the fifth-grade curriculum, would you please come forward and explain?"

L'Wren squeezes my knee. "Do not go forward."

"What am I supposed to do? She's looking right at me."

"Disappear. Fake a phone call. Faint. I don't know."

I raise my hand.

Lorraine points at me. "Yes . . . Um, remind me of your name?"

I have introduced myself to her during at least three different volunteer fairs. "Diana Wood." I stand at my chair, all heads swivel in my direction. "My daughter, Emmy, is in second grade."

"Okay," she says slowly. "So you have a young daughter and you are *not* concerned?"

"Well. Yes. Of course. I'm always concerned about Emmy. If there is a parenting thing to worry about, trust me, I've spent a sleepless night worrying about it. Sugar, screentime, hepatitis from a salad bar, *E. coli* from a lake." I laugh, a little too nervously, and L'Wren backs me up with a polite chuckle. "But I think sex education is valuable and needed in the curriculum and I can't help but notice a different problem."

"Which is?"

"Leave it." L'Wren coughs.

"I think we're talking about eliminating the very thing that could help our girls. A safe space to learn about sex. For example, these fifth-grade girls are already so focused on figuring out how to please boys. I think this kind of programming is a problem."

"Sorry?" Lorraine makes a meal out of looking confused.

My neck grows hot at her feigned confusion. "Not teaching them and keeping them in the dark isn't helping our girls. I mean, all of us here probably learned about blue balls by the time we were in middle school and thought they were a real thing." This gets a snicker from the room. "Because we didn't know better. It seems important for everyone to learn about their own bodies before worrying so much about gaining experience. And pleasing boys."

"Oh Jesus," L'Wren mumbles.

"I'm so confused." Lorraine shakes her chestnut bob. "Are y'all as confused as me? 'Diana,' is it?"

"Yes."

"Diana, your problem isn't that these young girls were discussing a sexual act that they are clearly too young to understand, but rather, that they were discussing the wrong sexual act. Am I getting this right?"

"Please sit down." L'Wren tugs at my skirt as another loud plane passes overhead. I'm sure L'Wren is hoping it'll land on us all. "I can't save you from this one, Diana. Please . . ."

"This is all to say . . ." My confidence falters. "I vote no on removing sex ed from the curriculum. Thank you so much for hearing me out."

The rest of the meeting goes by in a blur. I can only pay attention to my heart pounding too loud in my chest.

On our way to my car later, and safely out of earshot, L'Wren starts in on me. "What were you thinking? As if it's not all hard enough. As if we don't already feel like we're never doing enough and nothing will ever be good enough, and then you go and make enemies with Tracy Flick?"

"It's ridiculous. That whole meeting was insane."

"Diana, you've been at this school long enough, don't act so surprised." Safely in my car with the doors shut, she continues, "Last year the Parents League tried to ban Judy Blume from the school library. Not even a mildly racy one. *Superfudge*. They lost that battle, remember? And they'll lose this one, too, in the end. But don't pick a fight in public with that bully. Promise me. Not with everything you have . . . going on."

"You're not okay with what I'm doing, are you?"

"I don't know what it is! It's all been so hush-hush, remember? You barely even told me about it."

At the red light where I should be turning right toward L'Wren's house I say, "Come to the Dirty Diana office."

"Why?"

"Just come with me. For a visit."

"What if I don't want to?"

"Do you?"

"A little."

As we enter the office space, L'Wren covers her eyes and calls, "Is everyone dressed?"

But it's only Lou up front, who looks up from the reception desk with a baffled expression.

"She's with me," I apologize. I take L'Wren by the hand and we nearly smack into Petra as she's leaving.

"Perfect timing!" I say. As I introduce them they size each other up in a quick swallow.

"Love your Birkin," Petra coos.

"Love yours! I didn't know it came in such a beautiful blue."

"It doesn't."

I'm not used to seeing L'Wren outshopped, which only seems to turn her on.

"You don't need one, darling. You're perfect," Petra tells her. She gives L'Wren's shoulder a gentle squeeze and disappears, leaving L'Wren rattled.

"Was she flirting with me?"

"Kinda? But it's also how she talks. Do you want to see Liam's office?"

"He has an office?"

Liam's space is orderly as usual; today the only clutter is pinned to his bulletin board, an array of the prosthetic scars he makes alongside a severed finger.

He looks up at us in the doorway and grins. "As I live and breathe . . ."

"It's so tidy."

Liam catches my eye. "That's code for 'small.'"

"No. Tidy is tidy. It's nice."

"Thank you."

"You, however, desperately need a haircut."

"There she is!"

"I can get you with Stephan this Saturday if you're up before noon."

Liam's jaw tightens, and I loop my arm through L'Wren's. "Let me show you the rest of the place . . ." I give her a tour of the soundproof room where I record the interviews, then onto the common room where I like to paint near the big windows. I introduce her to Lynnie and Max, and then Lou takes her coffee order.

"Can I show you my favorite part?" I lead her to my office, a small sunny space near the back.

"What are these?" L'Wren stops in front of the many notecards taped to my wall.

"Abbreviated fantasies. Fans of the site have been sending in fantasies and we post clips of them on our social."

"These are all from different women?"

"A few months ago, there were only a handful . . ."

She studies the wall, reading each one, her eyes occasionally going big, but always smiling. "Oh, this woman likes feathers . . . And yarn? Huh. This gal is fantasizing about her daughter's boyfriend. That won't end well. Jesus, Diana, there are hundreds here. They're all so honest. It's amazing how they trust you with all this."

L'Wren takes in all the marketing materials scattered around and the photos of me for *Vogue*. After a slow lap, she takes a seat in a club chair by the open window with her decaf latte.

"I didn't expect it to be so . . . welcoming? Or maybe bright? And the women in your office are so put together. I'm impressed. If it weren't for Liam's scruffy haircut, I'd think you were working at a regular office—" She tries again. "You know what I mean. It's real. It's a whole operation. Honestly, since I've known you, you've had a boring finance job, which never seemed like it made sense for you. And the few times you talked about how you used to paint, your whole face would light up. And then you'd change the subject. So I get it." She looks up at me as if in apology before her eyes come to rest on the photos of me. "But I guess I wonder, do you have to be the face of it?"

"I do the interviews and the paintings. It's my voice. Don't you think it would be strange if it weren't me out there?"

"Maybe it would add to the mystery? Like Dear Abby? I don't think any of us believe that teeny picture in the paper is really her. It's probably a hundred different people giving us advice—" L'Wren looks down at her lap, then back at me. "Diana. Think of all the moms at our school who read *Vogue*. And really, it only takes one before everyone is gossiping. I just want you to think about it."

"I am. I will. I promise."

"Okay. And I've changed my mind. About you telling Oliver. Not because of any gossip. But because, look at all this. This is a real part of your life. He needs to know about it."

"Thank you."

She takes the last sip of her coffee. "Can we go now?"

"You're still uncomfortable?"

"There are seven different-colored vibrators on your desk."

I follow her gaze to the vibrator prototypes, neatly lined up next to my laptop.

"Would you like to try one?"

"No, thank you." For the first time today, her cheeks go pink.

"L'Wren?"

"Hmmmm?"

"You have used a vibrator before, haven't you?"

She crinkles her nose. "I was always too terrified someone would find it. Like in the movies."

"You could keep it somewhere safe."

"Those stores intimidate me."

"Buy one online."

"With weird names that show up on your credit card bills?"

"Like 'Amazon'?"

"Okay, but then what happens to my algorithm?" She sighs. "It's just not for me."

"But you have given yourself an orgasm?"

"Diana! Just because you've become a sex guru doesn't mean everything is on the table. I grew up in a house where it was unladylike to discuss these things."

"But you always told me about you and Kevin."

"That was nothing. All the details were what we all know. Calendar sex."

"Did he make you come?"

She doesn't answer, just purses her lips.

"Take the blue one. Please. Promise me you will try it."

"I'm not taking a vibrator."

"As a favor. Valuable research for a new product."

"I haven't. Okay?" Then, dropping into a stage whisper with her eyes glued to the door. "I haven't had an orgasm. I don't think I can. They just don't happen for me. It's not how I'm built."

"L'Wren—"

"Don't. I know, I grew up reading *Cosmo* too. Maybe I just need to try this, maybe your partner doesn't know how to blah blah blah."

"What about with Arthur?"

"I fake it. Just to take the pressure off."

Kirby knocks on my door with a question, and L'Wren relaxes back into her chair. I excuse myself and promise to drive her home in five minutes. When I come back to collect her, we scoop up our purses and head for the door. I glance back at my desk, delighted to see the blue vibrator is gone.

I want sex to be fun again. I want to be on a roller coaster about to fly down the steepest drop and have my boyfriend inside me. I want to stay up all night dancing and collapse into bed with just enough energy to fuck. I want my boyfriend to take me aside at a party for a quickie in the host's bedroom. I just want sex to be fun again.

Chapter Seven

To the surprise of us both, Oliver coaxes me onto the Ferris wheel at the Denton Spring Carnival. Our dates are happening with more frequency. Oliver has confessed to his parents that we are "spending time together again," and Emmy is thrilled to be spoiled by her grandparents on Saturday nights.

A teenager in bottle-thick glasses tears our tickets and waves us on. Oliver smiles and takes my hand, leading us to an empty bucket seat. The metal is cool through my jeans.

"Are you cold?" Oliver asks.

"Just nervous. This isn't how we go, right? On a rusty Ferris wheel in Denton?"

Oliver looks at me searchingly. "If anything, it will be on that Tilt-A-Whirl." The ride starts with a hard jerk. Soon we're high enough that I can see all the way from the funnel cake stand to the teacups and beyond, to the sea of cars in the parking lot.

"Remember when we used to make out on the roof of your old apartment building?" Oliver asks. "We were way higher up."

"That was me trying to impress you."

Inches from the top, we come to a stop so sudden that we're both thrown against the safety bar. "Someone must be getting on," Oliver murmurs.

He peers over the bar and our bucket sways. I grab him by the arm just as the ride moves, then stutters again. From below, someone shouts. "Rex! Where's that button?"

I lean into Oliver, and he puts his arm around me. "How can I take your mind off this?" he asks.

"Should we call the fire department?"

"Rex down there has got this. I promise."

I take a deep breath—the night air smells like funnel cake and gasoline—but it's cool and soothing. "Tell me a secret. Something you've never told me before."

The Ferris wheel sputters but only moves forward an inch or so. Some of our fellow passengers scream profanities at the kid in the glasses who seems to have given up. "Hey, asshole! Let us off!"

Then another passenger screams at the first screamer. "Watch your fucking mouth. I have kids here!"

Oliver laughs.

"No laughing!" I say. "Too much moving!"

Oliver takes my hand in his and gently kisses my fingers. I smile and will myself to relax. Maybe we are meant to be right here. Right now.

"Okay," he says. "The handcuffs aren't my only fantasy."

"Oh?"

"I might have lied to you about not being attracted to Jackie Gersh."

"Who?"

"Our neighbor. On Duvall Street. I dreamt a lot about having sex with you and other people when we were first married."

"Really?"

He nods. "Someone watching us. Someone you liked. Someone I liked."

"Another couple?"

"No. . . . Maybe. Like watching you get pleasure from someone else. I'm not sure how far I thought it through, but the dreams turned me on."

"But you don't think about it anymore?"

"Well," he says, smiling, "I haven't completely let go of the idea. But lately, I've just been dreaming about you. Thinking about you. Thinking about the things I want to do to you and with you."

His leg brushes mine. I want him so desperately in that moment. I think about his hands on my body, his breath on my neck. I feel addicted to thinking about these things—and I'm having trouble remembering ever having felt this dopey over Oliver. It's such a rush.

I grin up at him. Maybe this is my fantasy. Sitting on a broken Ferris wheel having an unexpected conversation with the person I was once so sure I knew inside and out, but who now seems new. "I'd kiss you right now but I think that'll make us sway." I rest my cheek against his shoulder instead.

At the beginning of our marriage, if I had known Oliver fantasized about having sex with me and other people, would I have helped make that fantasy a reality for him? Or would it have made me scared? Ashamed? Jealous? Maybe Oliver wasn't the only one keeping part of himself hidden in our marriage. For so long, I've been afraid of the secrets we've kept. But now I'm wondering if those secrets are what will hold us together. Maybe it's everything I've been working on at Dirty Diana. Maybe the newfound honesty between us will create a better foundation. Not the first house, not the baby, not even the first kiss. We're only now starting to build something strong enough to carry the weight of our marriage.

"Diana?"

"Yeah?"

"Tell me something real."

An invitation. This is the moment to tell him about Dirty Diana. But as I lift my head and turn to him, the Ferris wheel creaks to life with a quick, terrifying thrust. There is the sound of metal against metal and a brief silence followed by cheers.

Oliver and I both exhale; the solid ground is near. But this impending sense of safety is no competition for my cowardice. I hold Oliver's hand a little tighter and tell him a truth but not a secret. "I'm really happy to be dating my husband again."

Chapter Eight

I meet Petra for lunch in the Arts District. I spot her from across the street, sitting at the restaurant's window. When I join her at the table, she looks caught. She sits up tall and paints on a smile.

"Everything okay?"

"Of course. Have a drink," she says.

"Uh-oh. Are we celebrating or commiserating?"

"Absofuckinglutely."

I laugh. "Okay. Fine."

"You might not have noticed but the table is set for three."

"Liam?"

"Seriously? Liam would hate this place."

Men in suits. White tablecloths and too much cutlery. "True.

Someone you're dating?" I raise my eyebrows, and then—so quick it almost didn't happen—her smile falters then returns.

She laughs. "I'm not ready to date. Just fucking." A waiter brings us each a Bloody Mary. "How's the *Vogue* Q&A coming?"

"Almost finished," I lie.

"Great. Well . . ." She leans in and pats my hand. "As you know, we are on the receiving end of more and more calls and requests to share on the site. And one of those incoming calls—" She stops midsentence and beams at a spot just over my shoulder. In an instant, every other diner in the restaurant swivels a head in the same direction. "Here she is! Perfect timing."

I turn and recognize her immediately. "Natalie Hutton? She's our lunch date?"

Petra doesn't hear me. She's already standing to greet the gazelle headed toward our table.

Natalie Hutton is Hollywood royalty. Beloved by men and women, she's won two Oscars and can seemingly do anything, from dramas to musicals. Now she runs her own production company known for scooping up the film rights to every big new book.

Years ago, Oliver and I went to our first dinner party at L'Wren's where a very loud woman named Maisie asked us all, with the intensity of a popular eighth grader high on her own cleverness, "Who's your hall pass? Let's go around the table!" All around us, eyes twinkled while Oliver sunk into his seat and whispered in my ear, "Who should I say?"

I searched for an obvious, palatable name. "Natalie Hutton?"

"You must be Diana . . ." Natalie holds me by the shoulders and squeezes. "You're stunning."

"Oh. Thank you." She's even more beautiful in person than onscreen. Her skin glows, and her eyes sparkle. Her head seems a tiny bit big on her delicate frame, but this only makes her more mesmerizing. "You're gorgeous too," I stammer.

Petra smiles. "Yes, yes, we're all very attractive. Really. Sit, sit."

Natalie settles in and confides, "I was so nervous on the car ride here. I never get nervous. Ever."

"What about?" Petra asks.

"Meeting you two, of course!"

"Us?" I ask. "That can't be true."

"Are you calling me a liar?" The smile completely slips from her face.

"No!"

"I'm kidding!"

Petra laughs and I try to.

"Petra has told me so much about you. About your story. And I'm really just so inspired."

"She's inspiring."

"Can I gush?" Natalie leans in so close to me our foreheads are practically touching. "Who was it? Maybe my hairstylist, Trish. She finds everything before everyone else. She played one of your interviews for me while I was in her chair. And there was something about it. I don't know. In this business everything is so artificial. We're all trying so hard to be authentic and real and we can't, really. I was very impressed."

"Thank you. That's great to hear."

"I love that not all the fantasies are overtly sexy. At least for men. I played one for Ryan onset and he looked at me like, what? And I said it's not *for you*. It's for *me*.

"We're supposed to be so many things at all times. And especially in bed. Demure. Virginal. A tiger. We're supposed to like sex but not talk about sex. I'm in town shooting a romance. They're making those again by the way. And the director, I kid you not, pans the camera down as soon as my costar and I start to kiss. As if sex was inconsequential. Not an actual part of the story. But with any marriage, or dating, or fuck buddies, sex is a crucial, emotional part of the story. It says so much about who we are. What our trust level is. Where we are in the relationship. And he just glosses right over it. Really. I mean, the pan down? Might as well put Vaseline on the lens. Sorry. I'm oversharing. I do that when I'm nervous. My publicist's ears are burning somewhere. She's constantly biting her nails in the background."

"We love oversharing here." Petra smiles.

"I want you to interview me," Natalie says to me.

"For the site?"

"Yes. I want to share a fantasy. I think it's so important to enter the conversation in a real sex-positive way. Is that why you started Dirty Diana?"

"I was definitely feeling a disconnect with my own life," I tell her.

"Was that when you were living on the farm? I'm just trying to get in your head. I do that."

"The farm?"

Petra squeezes my knee under the table. "You know. When you were working on your parents' farm? Across from your father's Baptist church."

"The church?"

Petra stands. "I need the loo. Come with me?"

She practically yanks me up and out of my chair, dragging me behind her. In the restroom, as she reapplies her lipstick, I gape at her, unsure whether to laugh or panic. "The farm?"

"I can't believe she brought that up. I told her you don't like talking about that time in your life."

"What time? My Baptist era?"

"I had to sell you. You know, every publicist takes some liberties. We're selling a world. Your story." Petra wears her usual, unflappable look as she fixes her lipstick in the mirror. "She's even more gorgeous in person, isn't she?"

"What exactly did you tell her?"

"It wasn't her. It was on a call I had with her agents and I think even they might have embellished a little."

"About which part?"

"That you were maybe a little more smalltown-religious-repressed? Churchgoing, had cows-as-friends-growing-up kind of thing."

"Petra. I grew up in Los Angeles. In the Valley."

"The Valley." Petra pretends to shudder. "Not that far off, is it?"

"Um. I'm certainly not Loretta Lynn."

"A coal mine! Dammit. That could have worked." She blots her lips then turns to me. "I'm kidding. Diana. Don't look so serious. Isn't everything we do in life performative? That's the lesson I'm learning as I age." She turns back to the mirror, pulls at her face, sweeping everything up to her ears in the bathroom mirror. "Even the 'authentic' bits. It's all performance, really. It's the gist of your story that matters—after so many years, you began painting again, making art, connecting with other women. Who cares where it all started? Hollywood loves what it loves. Especially the heartbreak of a Texas woman worth rooting for." Even at lunch with a professional actress, Petra steals the show.

She turns and fixes my hair, smoothing down the layers around my face. "Just enjoy lunch. These things rarely go any further. Let alone lead to an actual film getting made. Wouldn't you like to have the undivided attention of a celebrity for an hour?" Petra's eyes sparkle. "Oooh, maybe *that's* your fantasy."

I do have fun with it. Back at the table, we spend the next hour laughing and telling stories, and three Bloody Marys later, Natalie is all eye contact. She leans in as I tell her about the beginnings of Dirty Diana and my first attempts at interviewing people. And then a flash from a camera startles us. Outside the window, a large bearded man in a beanie furiously snaps pictures of Natalie.

"Seriously?" She rolls her eyes. "Shit. Sorry."

In the few seconds it takes me to figure out what is happening, she apologizes again. "I didn't think paparazzi would follow me from the set." Then a well-dressed woman, who must have been near the host stand this entire time, materializes and takes Natalie by the elbow. She calls to me on her way out, "You'll interview, right? We'll find a time this week. I'm obsessed. Honestly."

And with that, she's gone. The table feels suddenly empty. The vodka, the blur of her departure, something is giving me an uneasy feeling.

Petra asks for the bill. She squeezes my hand, excited. "Those pics will be everywhere if we're lucky. Everyone will be wondering who you are."

Of course—that's the uneasy feeling.

"Do not freak out. Please do not freak out."

"L'Wren." Back in my car, I press the phone closer to my ear. "You can't say that and expect someone not to freak out. Are you all right?"

"I'm fine. Everyone is fine. But okay. Freak out. It's warranted."

"What happened?"

"Lorraine knows about Dirty Diana."

In the morning, I park next to L'Wren and we walk the girls into school together. As Emmy and Halston skip ahead, L'Wren opens the link to the petition on her phone. There are four signatures so far: Lorraine's, of course. Raleigh, and Tristan's mom, which is to be expected. She's Renfield to Lorraine's Dracula. But Hilary Ballard is the biggest surprise. "She's always been jealous of you," L'Wren says. "Remember when you got curtain bangs and she showed up in carpool with the exact same cut, but hideous, three days later? She's obsessed with you."

"How did Lorraine even find out about Dirty Diana?"

"Oh god. There she is." We both steal a glance at the entrance where Lorraine stands in her blazing yellow sundress and crisp white blazer, guarding the main entrance like a gargoyle. Raleigh gives her a quick hug before disappearing inside.

"Well . . ." L'Wren sighs. "There's the evidence. Hat Lady must have used what she knew about Dirty Diana to sidle up to Lorraine. This school is worse than Anne Boleyn's court!"

Raleigh carried that much of a grudge against me? Where do people get the time?

"Well"—my voice trembles—"I'm not going to be scared to show my face at school."

I wave goodbye to Emmy and turn to face Lorraine. "Good morning."

"Diana. Can we talk for a minute?"

L'Wren shoots me a look to ask, *Should I come with?*

"I'll call you later," I tell her.

When Lorraine leads me over to the bike racks I can't help but smile. But if she puts it together we're at the scene of the original crime, she says nothing.

"Diana, hon. I'm not the type of person to avoid confrontation. I say what is on my mind and I'm always honest. I tell my children to do the same." Her arms are folded across her chest as if I might be a physical threat.

"Thank you?"

"So in full disclosure, I did start a petition to have your family expelled from St. Mary's. But truly, it's not personal."

"Then why is my name on the petition?"

"What I mean is, it's not about you per se. I have no beef with you. I barely know you. I would start a petition for any parent who created pornographic material." Over Lorraine's shoulder a group of parents do a terrible job of pretending not to stare. "We're a close-knit school community, Diana. Right? Isn't that what you've always loved about St. Mary's?"

She leaves me no room to answer before barreling on. "And one parent's actions have a ripple effect, you understand? I've been on the site, Diana. I know what it is. The kids at St. Mary's look to us to be their role models. How does Emmy feel about what you do?"

Until now, I have felt surprisingly calm. But when she mentions Emmy's name it's like she's pulled a knife. Anger creeps up my neck. "I haven't told Emmy. I don't think she's old enough."

"Well, finally. We agree on something. Huzzah!" She cracks a smile, a mouthful of white, shiny Chicklet teeth.

"When she is old enough to understand, I think she will be supportive."

"Diana, *please*. Don't be naïve. She'll be humiliated."

I dig my fingernails into my palms. I can't remember disliking someone this intensely. "You could have done this a different way, Lorraine. We could have talked about this."

"Like we did at the meeting? When you gave your Vagina Monologue? Please."

Every time she says "please" it grates on me more. She goes on, "We approach life very differently."

"We do."

"I just don't see how there will ever be a common ground, do y'all? And I think, honestly, most parents will side with me."

I walk quickly back to my car, my head down in case I start crying. I slam the door shut and drive. The panic comes swiftly.

At first, it's just a feeling of lightness. Like I could float away if not for my seatbelt. Not a terrible sensation on its own. But when I grip the steering wheel and try to ground myself, the feeling only intensifies. *Pay attention. You're driving. Come back.* But I can't get back into my body. If I can't control my body, how do I control the car? I panic. My palms sweat. I think about swallowing until all I can think about is swallowing. Am I swallowing enough? *Feel your feet in your shoes, feel the pinch of your pants at your waist.* My eyes burn with tears. I pull over just so I can close them. *Come back.* I swallow and try and fail to catch my breath.

Miriam's wearing jeans and it's throwing me. I sit on her couch alone, no Oliver.

"Thanks for seeing me so last minute," I say calmly.

Miriam seemed to hear it in my voice as soon as she answered my call. On my way to her, I turned it all over and over again. What if Oliver had taken Emmy to school today? Would Lorraine have approached him for a signature? How could I think Dirty Diana would stay a secret until I suddenly felt like telling him? I was so naïve, like a child playing hide-and-seek behind a broom. They'll never find out it's me!

"Diana, I don't typically see individuals on their own, when I'm working with them as a couple. If you need a referral for someone—"

"It will just be this once. I needed to talk with someone who knows us both."

"I can't keep this from Oliver."

"I know. I don't want you to."

I tell Miriam everything. From the start of Dirty Diana back in Santa Fe, to interviewing women in my office after work, to now, with Petra's money and our own offices. She lets me talk, never taking a single note or interrupting me with a question. When I do finally fall silent, she sits up in her chair, crosses and recrosses her legs, not saying anything for what feels like a very long time. When she does finally speak, it's more of an exhale. "Well."

"I'm ready to tell him. I want to tell him. We're in a good place."

"You've been waiting to tell him until, when? When you felt you could predict his reaction?"

"Sort of?"

"And you felt that his reaction would be one that made you feel closer instead of pushing you away?"

"We've been changing and moving in all the right directions, toward intimacy, but there is this small part of me . . ." I'm lying. A very big part of me. ". . . That is scared this will ruin it."

"Why?"

"Because he'll feel like he can't trust me. Like I've kept something secret from him for so long."

"Didn't he also keep secrets from you?"

"Yes, but we've moved past that. Poker was never poker. It feels like ages ago already."

"But this lie feels like something you can't move past?"

"This lie is tied to who I am. A part of me."

"Diana, you are not dirty."

My eyes fill with tears.

"And your worry about lies, and which ones you can survive . . . Isn't this version of a relationship you are protecting with Oliver the biggest lie of them all?"

Chapter Nine

On Saturday night, I change three times before Oliver arrives to pick me up, as if choosing the right outfit will make this evening go more smoothly.

Ten minutes into our drive to see a Memphis band who Oliver loves but has never seen live, he gets a call that a pipe has burst at the house he's renovating. The contractor onsite tries to reassure him that he took care of it before he left and he'll see him there on Monday.

"Do you mind? It's on the way."

At first, there are only trees—towering, sleepy river birch lining the driveway. We pull closer and the hidden midcentury home comes into view. By the time we've pulled into the open carport, I'm in love. Even with all its bruises and disrepair on display, it looks so regal, sitting in the wooded grove.

"Oliver. It's beautiful."

He takes my hand and leads me across a wooden footbridge, uneven and missing planks, but sturdy enough to carry us over a fast-moving creek.

As he pulls out the keys, I think about our house. The one we moved into just before Emmy was born. That house knew exactly who it wanted us to be: newlyweds with an open kitchen and a guest room for the mother-in-law. And so did the house next door. And the one next door to that. And the one across the street. The week we moved in, I caught myself walking up the wrong driveway twice.

"You'll get used to it," my friendly neighbor told me. "Maybe you should paint your mailbox. That could help?"

I took his advice and painted it deep purple, a color I was sure no one else would choose. It made me happy every time I pulled up. But the Neighborhood Association felt differently. There was a list of approved mailbox colors and purple wasn't one of them. So I painted it gray again and left a single purple dot on top. A small act of defiance.

Inside Oliver's flip, we move from room to room but it feels more like floating—the space is light and airy, with cedar beams and skylights. The construction is in progress, and the exposed wiring and unfinished drywall only add to the charm of the place—you can see the work and care going into it.

When we get to the dining area, I give a delighted gasp. "I would paint in this room every afternoon."

"Come here. I want to show you my favorite part." Oliver leads me to a screened-in porch off the kitchen. In the center of the room, a tree has grown up through the floorboards.

"We're doing everything we can to save it."

"You have to." I run my hand down the trunk.

"I want to honor everything, you know? The original design. I'm not looking to change anything, just bring it back to life. It might kill me, but I think it will be worth it."

We stand in silence, admiring the room. Then he takes me by the hand again and leads me to the primary bedroom. He describes what he wants to do in detail, but the more he lights up, the more I begin to panic. I want to enjoy it, but I can't. My hand grows clammy in his.

"I have to tell you something."

"Okay." He looks suddenly as nervous as I feel.

"It's big. It's something I've been keeping from you."

I drop his hand and sit on the floor in the middle of the empty room. I pull my knees close to my chest.

Oliver sits beside me. "I can hear whatever it is. It's me."

"I've been painting. More than ever. Drawing, painting, charcoal and oils, all of it."

"That's great, Diana." He narrows his eyes. "Did you think that would bother me?"

"I'm painting women I interview. About their erotic fantasies." I tell Oliver all about the site, never taking my eyes off him. His face is neutral, except for the crease between his eyes—it's a familiar expression, the same one he's always had when he's listening intently. "It's a business now, really. One that's starting to make money."

"Oh." He leans back on his hands and studies me. "You played me one once . . ."

"Yes. I did."

"And my reaction . . ." We're remembering the same night, when I had played him a snippet of a recording. The same night he told me he was falling out of love with me.

"Is that why you were nervous to tell me now? Because of that night?"

"Things have been so tenuous with us for so long, and now they're still tenuous but promising-tenuous? I don't want to trip us up again."

"Who else knows?"

"A lot of people will know. Very soon. And they'll know it's mine."

"But who in your life already knows?"

"L'Wren. Liam. Petra." I think about Lorraine and her petition. Raleigh. "Some moms at the school found out."

"Can I see it?"

"Of course." When he doesn't take his eyes off me, I add, "Now?"

He nods and I pull up the site on my phone. Oliver takes in all the portraits, the dozens of women's names.

"These are all your paintings? When did you record all the interviews?"

"Some I recorded before we split up. Some are more recent."

"I still don't get it. Why didn't you tell me?"

"I want to be open but I'm also scared to break the spell we're under."

"Can you give me a minute?"

His voice is flat, giving me little clue. The more neutral his expression, the more I feel the blood drain from my face. "Of course."

Oliver takes my phone and shuts himself inside the bathroom. I can hear him lean against the closed door and picture him sliding to the floor. I mirror him so that we're sitting back-to-back. He presses play. We listen to the first interview together. For the first few minutes, I hear him shifting his weight against the door. Finally he settles in and the only sound is Natalie's voice, fantasizing about reuniting with someone she met when she was young and broke.

. . . I had a job at the airport. I was nineteen, and I'd get up every morning at 4 A.M. to take two buses to be there in time to open up the coffee kiosk. Miserable passengers headed for their cramped coach seats after having made it through the snaking lines of check-in are delirious to get their first coffee of the day, even if it's just weak-ass drip coffee like I was pouring. I'd warm my frozen fingers on the handle and make their day. With the coffee. And with me. They're up so early and they're not expecting to see someone as good-looking as I was then, someone who the shitty uniform can't hide the shape of, someone who rolled out of the shower with wild curls that you couldn't pay the most expensive hairdresser to achieve. And so with that drunk-on-sleeplessness feeling, the passengers would take me in, amazed. Dads with their screaming kids. Honeymooners—a newlywed scornfully pulling their man away from me. Teenage boys with their moms. Whole soccer teams. They'd stammer and stare. I'd have to ask them to speak up when they gave

me their order. Who the hell gets intimidated by a teenage girl working at the airport below minimum wage? Well, that's what beauty does. I can see that now that I'm older. Beauty changes things. It did for me too.

  One day, there was a new chef standing over a griddle, and he was absolutely smoking. I felt, from the first dawn I laid eyes on him, how the dads must have felt when they'd arrive and see me pouring their coffee. His name was Will, he was twenty-three and wandering between jobs. He had black hair, high cheekbones, a long bony nose, and black-lashed green eyes. His sinewy arms rippled with homemade tattoos. He said he was Cherokee but I don't know, it's what a lot of white trash boys where I'm from say when they want to be something bigger, when they want to assign a beauty to the poverty they're trapped in. Will was quiet, but he'd touch my hips, as if by mistake, as if I were a piece of furniture, as he moved across the tiny kitchen. The first time he did it, I swear to God, I felt like I was gonna come. If one of the Coffee Dads had tried to fuck me in the bathroom I'd probably had done it, so overwhelming was the hot feeling between my legs by the end of my shift. The next day I tried harder than ever to engage Will in conversation but, politely, he rebuffed me, barely looked at me so that when he did occasionally make eye contact—sudden, unwavering—I tried not to audibly gasp. I thought about asking him to give me one of his shitty tattoos just to have his fingers on me. The first time he really talked to me, there was a line and some rich asshole had cut to the front. "I'm in a rush" he snapped at a single mom with her yelling toddler. Then he saw me and he wasn't in such a rush. Then he had time to chat and he was holding up the line. "Make me a latte, sugar tits." Will heard what he'd said and stepped in from the kitchen and asked, "Is there a problem here?" His voice was deep, which I'd barely registered as he spoke so little. He and the asshole went back and forth, seemed to be squaring up for a fight. Then the asshole's final flight announcement was called and he went on his way, having served his purpose—getting Will to talk to me. Getting Will I hoped, finally, to at least take note of my tits. He put his hand on my shoulder, asked, "Are you okay?" I said I was, that it happened to me a lot, I was used to it, hoping he'd get the message and pursue me. But he just shrugged and went back to the kitchen.

I've had so many men since then. But I never did have Will. Just the memory of his hands on my hips as he passed me in the kitchen. Of him asking, one time, "Are you okay?" So here's my fantasy: the boy from the lowest point of my life, high in the air with me on my private plane. Better yet, it's a plane the studio loaned me for my own private use to try and get me to sign on to some dumb project. Even though I'm in a plush leather chair, I'm back in my uniform from the coffee stand. I have no idea why he's on the plane with me. It's not because I impressed him. No—Will is the captain, he's flying the plane! "You made it, Will!" I say, when I see him in the cockpit. "Yup." "And this was what you always wanted? I had no idea. You were so hard to read." He turns around, hands it over to his copilot who, it turns out, is a very safe pilot even though he's the guy who'd owned the coffee stand.

Will closes the cockpit door and walks toward me. Stunned, I sit down in my seat, or lie down on it since someone has made it up into a double bed. "What I always wanted," he answers, "was you."

"You could have had me any day!"

"But I couldn't have kept you. I knew you were going places. I knew you were a bill I couldn't afford to pay."

Will rolls the fabric up my thighs and soon his thick, tattooed fingers are inside me. The dads from the coffee stand are watching, the teenage boys are watching. Then Will unbuckles his cheap belt and lets me see his cock for the first time, as luxurious as we were broke. The airport honeymooners are sucking off their new husbands while they watch us. He wraps my long legs around his tan shoulders as he slides inside for the very first time after decades of waiting. "Are you okay?" Will asks as he thrusts inside me. He was never a built guy but turns out all the weight he's been carrying is in his cock. And after he's made me explode, and we've touched down in London for my premiere, I carry that feeling with me all day, through press and then on the red carpet. How warm he made me feel, then and now, that feeling of the one boy who didn't collapse with need in front of me, that feeling of flying far, far away.

Oliver plays another one. I'm on a train. It's dusk, and through the window I can see . . .

And then another one.

I hear my own voice, over and over again, asking questions.

And when that fantasy ends, he plays another.

. . . And once the show is over, his security guard finds me in the parking lot and leads me to his tour bus. He wants me to join him for the night.

Then it's quiet. Minutes pass before I hear Oliver stand, and so I do too.

The door finally opens. I don't want to be the first one to speak. "Diana . . ."

I meet his gaze. He circles my wrists with his fingers. "It's you. How could I not like anything that's you?" He leans close and kisses me. It's tender, full of the relief we both feel, both of us knowing there is no place we'd rather be than right here.

And then we can't hold back. Our clothes come off quickly, as if they were seconds from catching fire. Oliver's body has changed. He's stronger, his shoulders broader. I cover my breasts with my hands, suddenly feeling self-conscious.

But in an instant, our hands are all over each other, exploring the places we longed for and missed over the last year.

With his hands on the small of my back, Oliver lowers me to the floor, reaching for his sweater and placing it under my head. "Is this okay?"

All I can do is nod, my voice caught in my throat.

Oliver is on top of me now. And I can feel my body prepare for our familiar sex. But instead of immediately entering me, he slowly teases me with the tip of his erection. I moan in pleasure, letting him know that I love every second of it.

"Fuck me," I tell him. "Please." His sparkling eyes never leave mine as he finally enters me, slowly pushing deeper. I lift my head so I can watch our bodies coming together, dripping into each other.

Our lovemaking was always so tentative. Under covers or turned on our sides, both of us going through the motions. But now, I tighten around him. Are these the same bodies? Melting into each other in new levels of ecstasy?

My orgasm comes out of nowhere. Quick, pronounced pangs of pleasure each as short-lived as a struck match. "I'm coming," I moan and Oliver follows. And then it's over. I want to applaud. Congratulate us in some way.

"I'm sorry," he says, smiling, watching my own smile blossom. "I usually last longer."

"It's okay." I laugh. "I do too."

We lie on the hard wood floors, beneath the shiplap ceiling, our hearts racing. I wonder if my orgasms will always be so within reach? As impossible to stop as a runaway train.

"What next?"

"Well." He turns his head and smiles at me. "We lie to Miriam, of course."

"I mean it. What now, for us?"

"We do it again." He props himself on his elbow looking down into my eyes. "And again. And again. Until we both can't walk." He kisses me tenderly. We are both sticky with sweat and sex but I don't care. I pull him closer. It feels right to be in his arms.

"I think what you're building is really cool," he says.

"Cool?" We both grin.

"Great. Brave. Surprising."

Outside the giant windows, the last of the daylight fades. We watch the biggest of the live oak trees sway. If we lived here, this would be the view from our bed.

"Can I show you something?"

He kisses my neck. "Show me everything."

Beneath a pile of our rumpled clothes, I find my phone and show Oliver all the plans we have for the site. The press materials. The Q&A from *Vogue*.

"You haven't filled it out yet."

"I think I couldn't until you knew everything. I didn't want you to have to read about it in *Vogue*."

"I don't read *Vogue*."

"You know what I mean."

"Let's fill it out. This'll be fun."

"Together?"

"*Vogue* wants to know what you're thinking. So do I. C'mon." He sounds genuinely excited.

"And once the article comes out, it will be out. In the world. Your parents will be able to google it. Your friends can look it up." I watch him closely.

"I know."

"And?" I rest my head on his naked chest. His heart beats strong and fast.

"I don't know. We've been hiding for so long. I don't want to do it anymore. It's almost like you knew. Like you knew we had to blow up the life we had. And maybe this is what brings us together." He clears his throat and reads. "Where's your favorite place to wake up?"

"Could be here?"

"On a scale of one to ten, how excited are you about life right now?"

"Ten."

"If you could do a love scene with anyone, who would it be?"

"You."

"You don't have to say any of this."

"It's true."

"This isn't a *Vogue* question, but was that Natalie Hutton I listened to?"

"I just met her."

"Did you tell her she was my hall pass?"

"It didn't come up."

He pulls me closer, kissing my cheek. I can't remember ever having felt this connected to him, this open and easy. I look around the house he's building—the man who begrudgingly worked for his father seems so far away.

Oliver turns back to the questions. "What's one thing people don't know about you? Okay, well, I think we know the answer to this one."

"But people do know."

"How about that we almost got a divorce?"

"People will know that too."

"How?"

"It's all part of the story. Our story. Are you okay with that?"

"Will they know that we . . . stopped having sex and all that?"

"Yes."

"Right."

"Does that worry you?"

"It would worry my father."

"And you?"

Oliver lets out a long, slow exhale. "It's so boring to fear that you are unfuckable. So no. I'm going to say no. Your turn: What's your wake-up ritual?"

"An alarm and a deep, existential sigh?"

"What's your bedtime ritual?"

"Set the alarm with a deep, existential sigh?"

"What's your favorite time of day?"

"Dusk. Except when Emmy was a newborn and the sun setting filled me with bottomless anxiety about another sleepless night."

"I remember."

"I know."

I'm deep in the memory of those newborn days and us as new parents when he interrupts, "Heels or flats?"

"Hmm. Probing. Flats."

"What do you hope your tombstone will read?"

"What? This questionnaire is giving me whiplash."

"You have to answer."

"Says who?"

"Don't change the subject."

"Okay, okay." I look out into the now pitch-black night. I can feel Oliver watching me, trying to guess how I'll answer. I turn to him and say, 'Let's not stay the same.'"

He considers. "Wouldn't it be more like, 'Here lies Diana, she didn't stay the same'?"

I roll my eyes. "I'm being cremated anyway. Next question."

"Style icon?"

"Sadly, my mother. She has great style."

"I'd like to see Ava again. Give Emmy the chance to know her."

"Maybe." My mom met Emmy when she was a month old. After that first visit, we invited her to join us for Emmy's first Christmas, but she couldn't make it, something about an audition she couldn't miss. *Yes, over the holidays,* she'd insisted when I pressed.

We invited her for Emmy's first birthday, then her second. In the beginning, our invitations were followed up by excuses and then she stopped replying and we stopped inviting. Her phone calls weren't timed to birthdays or holidays, and they weren't peppered with "I miss you." Instead she'd say, "Something made me think of you, just saying 'hi.'" Occasionally, I'd wake up in the middle of the night, worried I hadn't heard from her and convinced something terrible had happened. She must be lying ill on the floor of her apartment; she'd been in a car accident, something awful. In the morning, when I called her, she would answer, sleepily, "Hey." As if months hadn't passed. As if we spoke every day.

Any feeling of relief I had was quickly replaced by a red-hot flush of anger. "Are you okay?" I'd ask.

"God no."

For a moment, my heart would race, I'd brace myself for terrible news. And then she would sigh. A long sigh. Then she would launch into a list of grievances the world had leveled against her—a flat tire, a petty casting director who for some reason was out to get her, a lousy date who stiffed her with the bill. She'd speak and the heat would spread through my body. I hated listening to all the ways the world had wronged her. And still, none of it ever felt so dire that she couldn't also make time for her granddaughter. By the time we hung up, my hands would be shaking in anger. I fell for it. For her. Again.

"She's part of you," Oliver says quietly.

"Just not the part I like."

"I like all parts of you." He kisses my shoulder and reads, "What's one ingredient you put in everything?"

"Garlic salt."

"Really?"

"Yes. Go on."

"What three people living or dead would you like to make dinner for?"

"Your great-grandmother. Joan Mitchell, the painter. And . . . come back to me."

"What's your biggest fear in life?"

"Going backward."

"Window or aisle seat?"

"Aisle."

"What's your secret talent?" Before I can answer Oliver offers, "Making erotica?"

"Painting."

"Most adventurous thing you've done in your life?"

"Making erotica," we answer in unison.

"Dolphins or koalas?"

"That's not seriously the question?"

"I swear."

"Red pandas."

"Blow-dry or air-dry?"

"Someone was getting tired of writing these . . ."

"We're almost done. Best thing to happen to you today?"

"Sex in this beautiful house."

"Worst thing to happen to you today?"

"Leaving this beautiful house."

"Best compliment you're ever received."

"'I still love you. It never went away. Even when I told you it had.'"

"Hey. I said that. Okay, last one. What is your fantasy?"

"Come back to it?"

"This one was written specifically for you. The finale."

"No pressure."

"You've interviewed so many women. You've never shared yours?"

"Sex on the floor of the midcentury house my husband is renovating?"

Oliver shakes his head in faux dismay. "Phoning it in." He tosses the quiz aside and rolls onto me, then pins my arms above my head. "Placating." He kisses my neck, down to my breasts. A shiver runs through my body. "I'll accept it." I feel his erection, hard and urgent, pressing into my thigh. "For now." He brushes the hair from my neck and kisses my bare skin. "But later, you'll tell me your real one."

Oliver kisses me all the way down to my stomach, parting my legs and kissing my inner thighs. I fight the reflex to close them. There are so many windows. There is nowhere to hide.

"I want to know what you like," he says.

"You know what I like," I tease.

"Not really."

I try to stay in the present. I don't want to remember that we never asked each other. That we tiptoed around sex as if it were an impolite topic. When we were in trouble, it felt like homework. But now, on the floor of this house, his chest hovering above me, it feels like an adventure we're embarking on together.

"Give me your fingers," I whisper. "Two."

He positions himself between my legs and I guide his hand to the opening of my vagina, which is already wet with anticipation.

"Slowly," I say.

He moves exactly as I tell him, entering me slowly with his fingers. My body wraps around him, thickening as he slides in and out of me.

"Oh, Diana," he says, as if letting him do this is the greatest gift I could give him. His erection presses against me, but he is only focused on me. He slides his fingers in and out of me, gliding them along my tender skin—each time they leave my body, my hips reach out for his touch again.

"You're so wet," he says, admiring every fold, every soft corner of me.

"Now rub my clit," I tell him, and his eyes light up.

"You want me to rub your clit?" he asks, showing me that he can say it too. That people can change. They can still surprise and delight you.

"Yes."

He uses his thumb to press into me. I'm a puddle now. He watches my every movement.

"Keep touching me," I tell him. Every word I say out loud gives me an unexpected charge. "Three fingers now."

He is deeper inside me. "Here?"

"Lower."

"Here," he says. My hips rise. "You like it when I do this?" He knows the answer. He just wants me to say it out loud.

"Yes."

He's stroking himself now. "Do you want me inside you?" He is still stroking us both.

"Yes."

He flips me over so my breasts are pressed against the floor. My body is so open, so ready for him.

"Tell me you need my cock," he breathes into my ear as he pushes in and out of me. The words coming out of Oliver's mouth make me spin. I lift myself up so I am on all fours and Oliver is kneeling behind me.

"Pull my hair," I tell him.

He grabs a handful of my hair and yanks it hard enough to make my head fall back. We're moaning together, pleasure coursing through us. My breasts, wet with perspiration, rise and fall as he plunges inside me, and I still need more. I want more pressure, more tension, more of this Oliver.

"I love your cock," I tell him. I can feel Oliver blush, heat radiating off his body. "I love it so much," I say.

And then he explodes inside me. "Keep going," I say, and he moves against me in and out until I cry out.

On Monday morning, Oliver and I sit in the cab of his truck, in the parking lot of Miriam's office, rehearsing our story.

"We had a fun time at the concert and drove home. I absolutely did not say 'I love your cock.' Not once," I instruct. It's fun to make him blush. Which he does.

"That's been my mantra all morning. I haven't stopped replaying it in my head."

"It's true." I beam. It is impossible not to recognize that we've slept with each other. We are like kids that absolutely did not just put a whoopee cushion under the teacher's seat.

Sharing the same observation, Oliver says "We should talk about a specific song maybe?"

"But what if they didn't play it?"

"You think she'll check the set list?"

We are half kidding/half serious and not wanting to be a disappointment to Miriam. "This is crazy," I say. "We should just sit down and ask her, 'Miriam, when can we have sex?'"

"No. She'll know we failed. We have to go in there and lie through our teeth."

"She'll tell us we're not ready."

"But we are ready. We were. We did. We have to tell her."

"You and I know we're ready, but she wanted us to date for much longer."

"We failed. Maybe we admit we failed."

Oliver pulls me into him and kisses me tenderly.

"Saturday did not feel like a failure. In fact, I've been thinking about it all morning."

"Our appointment is three minutes ago."

"What if we tell her we're planning to have sex on Friday. If all goes well. And then by our next appointment, we won't have to lie."

"Okay. Good plan."

We pull ourselves from the car and drift through the parking lot, careful not to walk too close or let any pieces of our bodies touch. When we both reach for the elevator button at the same time, Oliver quickly pulls his hand away like it's on fire. "Sorry," I mumble.

We smile gently, appropriately, when Miriam ushers us onto her couch.

We sit in unison.

And when she asks us how we're doing, we answer in unison.

"We had sex."

Chapter Ten

On a Monday morning in June, I pull into the parking lot at work, the same job I've had at my father-in-law's firm—McKinnon, Wood, and Bloom—for over fifteen years. I recognize every car and every crack in the asphalt. I count them on my way into the lobby, then drift through the air-conditioning all the way to my desk. I scroll through my inbox, decide what's most urgent then jump at a voice in my doorway. Allen.

"Diana. Glad I caught you. Follow me to my office?"

A question that is not a question.

I sit opposite his mahogany desk. The same deer I've avoided eye contact with for fifteen years stares from the wall behind Allen's head. He settles into his chair. "I'm not sure if you've been following the latest, but John Markham was photographed leaving a strip club on Friday. And again on Saturday."

"I missed that." I did see the headline, but I hadn't bothered clicking. Senator Markham was one of my favorite of Allen's clients, always making an effort to ask about my day and never asking me for a cup of coffee. A low-but-meaningful bar.

"Our firm, of course, can't be associated with that kind of behavior."

"Going to a strip club?" Three of our last five holiday parties have ended with an after-party at a strip club.

"It's all so public. With John's recent divorce from Melissa. Cheating allegations. No chance he'll win another term. He's losing his base."

"And his money."

"It was always her money, Diana. And one has to choose sides even when it hurts. It feels like the right time to part ways with John and shore things up with Melissa. You wouldn't mind letting him know, would you? You two are friendly."

"You want me to get rid of him as a client?"

"And take Melissa to lunch."

I don't care about Allen taking sides. Or following the money. Or the wild hypocrisy of dropping a client for moral reasons. Secretly I find it all entertaining. The same way that on the best of days, showing up at the office is entertaining. Reliably, we arrive and perform—we follow the script about what we should care about and not care about. And who's in charge and who's invited to a meeting. Who holds the door and who speaks first and who takes notes.

Some days I imagine it like we're dinner theater actors in some town starved for entertainment. We perform the same play again and again and pretend there is no audience. And some days showing up and knowing I didn't have to learn any new lines gives me a sense of peace and calm. I could do this show in my sleep. Until lately. As Allen speaks, the houselights come up and the audience is there. I can see them from the stage, tearing into their prime rib from the smorgasbord, looking up at me, expectantly.

"I don't think I can."

"Take her to lunch? You have something?"

"No." I sit in the chair opposite him so I won't chicken out and slip out the open door. "I was actually planning to find you today. Oliver has been earning solid money flipping houses—"

"Solid?"

"He's very good at it."

"And? What does this have to do with you?"

"I'm giving my notice, Allen."

The next twenty minutes feel otherworldly and light. I float back to my desk and type an official resignation letter. Then I pack up my picture frames and put the money plant from my windowsill into a box and decide to take myself for an early lunch, where I will make a list of everything I need to wrap up and delegate so I won't leave anything unfinished for Allen.

I weave through the maze of cubicles and think of the days spent here with Oliver—my immediate crush on him, our first kiss in the stairwell. Coming back to work after Emmy was born; the broken lock on my office door and having to shove a chair up against it so I could pump milk for Emmy without anyone walking in. I think of the nights just last year when I interviewed women in my office afterhours, praying no one would find out.

Thinking about Dirty Diana, my memories cascade into worry—what if the business isn't enough to support us? What if Oliver's next house doesn't sell? What if we're both out of work? By the time I reach my car, the cardboard box of my office bric-a-brac feels like it might crush me. I turn on the AC and catch my breath.

Then I dial Natalie Hutton's number. An assistant answers, and to my surprise she puts me through.

"I have an idea."

Natalie listens as I pitch her on a gallery show idea I've been dreaming up for months, only now I tweak it so that Natalie and her portrait are at the center of it all. When I stop talking, there's a long pause and for a moment I worry she's dropped off.

"I love it. Are you in L.A.?"

"No. But I can be." I just quit my job.

"Let me make a few calls and get back to you?"

I spend the entire afternoon emailing back and forth with Alicia, the two of us creating a pitch document for a Dirty Diana gallery evening with Natalie as the main draw.

Oliver comes by to drop off Emmy and I invite him to stay for dinner. Before I can tell him about quitting, he smiles and lets me know his mom already called. He opens a bottle of champagne and pours us each a glass.

While I'm cooking, I glance at my phone and see a string of texts from Petra:

Call me.

Seriously. Call me.

Diana. Call me back.

She picks up right away. "You will not believe this."

"Is everything okay?"

"I spent the entire evening on the phone with Natalie's agent, then her manager, then a team of film execs, including her producing partner, Allison Kidd, who wants you to come to Los Angeles and meet with her."

"Me? Why?"

"Because they want to produce Dirty Diana. To buy the IP and turn it all into a movie about your life journey."

"That wasn't the pitch."

"What do you mean that wasn't the pitch?"

"I called Natalie and pitched her the gallery idea. A very different idea."

"Finally! Thank god. You have no idea how long I've been waiting for this moment."

"What moment?"

"For you to fucking hustle!"

"Petra." I can't help laughing. "Is my life—even with the *Footloose* version of my childhood—interesting enough for a movie?"

"As your friend, I'd say, 'maybe?' But as your publicist, I'd say you're pitchable. Let's just get you in the room."

In the backyard, Oliver is watching Emmy practice her cartwheels. When I recount the strange call, he looks as confused as I feel. "A movie?"

"They say the actual making of the movie hardly ever happens. They just like to buy stuff up and then never make any of it."

"But it's about your life? Would I be in it?"

"Maybe a character based on you. What do you think?"

"I think it's exciting." He watches as Emmy runs off to find her sidewalk chalk. "And what about Jasper?"

I feel my ears go pink. "I don't know. I don't know how much would be real or fictional or what they would even find interesting about it. It's all way too soon to think about. No one has offered anything."

For a long while, we sit and watch Emmy draw a sweet, smiling bunny in pink chalk. And then something with fangs chasing the bunny. Oliver and I share a familiar look that says *she's adorable and weird and better than either of us and did we do okay have we done enough, so far?*

"I don't want any of this drama at school to affect Emmy," I say quietly.

"The parent Mafia? It won't." Oliver drapes his arm around me and pulls me close. He's warm, his body solid and comforting. "It'll blow over before summer's done and Lorraine will be on to a new crusade. She'll have fired a teacher and three janitors by fall and be totally sated."

Oliver cleans up the kitchen while I run Emmy a bath, trying to keep Oliver's reassuring voice in my head. Once she's asleep, I pull up the calendar on my phone and ask him, "School's out next week, so what if we picked up after that and went to California? I could take my meeting and we can vacation as well."

"The three of us?"

"It might be fun? Unless you can't get the time away?"

Oliver skims the calendar, reading over my shoulder. "It's actually perfect. The permit for the pool is being held up for at least a month, so things are at a temporary standstill at the house. What about Emmy's camp?"

"She'd have the beach. Disneyland? Lack of humidity and mosquitos? And don't forget, your parents will be in Santa Barbara for most of July. Maybe they could even take Emmy for a few days while we lie on a beach somewhere."

Oliver pulls me into his lap. "Yes." He's thinking what I am: It means we'd be living together again. Not saying goodbye at the end of a date. Spending all day and night together. "We need a reset. What better place than Hollywood?"

> *I've lived a full life. That's what you say, right? But it's true. A wonderful life that unfolded in order. When my husband proposed, we looked forward to the wedding. Then our first home. Then the first child, of course. A lovely daughter, with a gap-toothed smile. We had more children than we planned just to have that feeling of something big interrupting our lives. And now, the kids are all married and scat-*

tered across the country. We take trips, of course. We visit the kids. They send us on cruises because they think that's what we want. But we're still looking for that next big thing. In my fantasy, we start having sex in public places. At the park. On a bench at the museum. In the movie theater. Why not? We even make a pact: We will not die until we've had sex on the sundeck of a cruise ship.

PART TWO

*Los Angeles,
California*

Chapter Eleven

As our flight descends, I lean over Emmy at the window seat and watch the Los Angeles ground come up to meet us. It all looks so familiar—the endless sprawl of buildings, the Tic Tac houses in rows, the sapphire-blue swimming pools. It's late afternoon and the smog hugs the hills.

Everything about our trip to L.A. has fallen smoothly into place. Three nights ago, Petra and Oliver met for the first time over drinks. She took us to a dive bar in Garland that they'd both been to before, and they quickly bonded over their love of college football. And then, as if I weren't sitting beside them, they decided I am a good secret keeper but a terrible liar.

"The worst." They smiled in unison.

"Ha ha," was all I had to add. At which point they both worried they'd careened into hurting my feelings, and I assured them they definitely had not.

Oliver narrowed his eyes. "Well, I guess we'd know if she were lying."

We all laughed and Petra squeezed my knee. I could have stayed in the warm glow of the evening for hours. "I'm sorry, it's just so exciting to meet Oliver," she said. Then, like an expert publicist, she won us over with a new plan for our time in L.A. After realizing we would still be in Los Angeles for the Fourth of July, Petra decided it would be the perfect time to fly in herself and throw a Dirty Diana party. "A celebration! We'll bring L'Wren, Alicia, the whole staff. I'll invite Vibezz!"

I turned to Oliver, "Two z's." And to Petra, "Why are your eyes lit up like that?"

"It's perfect. The Vibezz founder wants to collaborate on the Dirty Diana vibrator, but why not bring them on as proper investors? My money is small fry compared to what a true investment could do for you."

"Are they interested?"

"Their interest is definitely piqued, but they want to meet you." She spent the next twenty minutes convincing us both that a party would be the perfect venue to woo them. Petra's ambition and money had gotten us off the ground, but for Dirty Diana to succeed, we needed help. As the reality of quitting my job sets in, so does the pressure of making Dirty Diana work—but it's also thrilling.

On the way home from the bar, we had called Oliver's parents and told them we had decided to vacation in Los Angeles. Allen only made one crack—"California? I thought a couple of retirees like you would be headed for Florida"—before insisting Emmy should spend the Fourth of July weekend with them an hour away in Montecito. They even offered to fly back to Dallas with her so Oliver and I could have a few extra days on our own.

Now, as the plane circles LAX, this kind of falling into place feels *too* easy. I wait for the first shoe to drop. *No. It's exciting. It's all exciting. You know this place. The view out the window is familiar.*

But so is the dread. It climbs up the back of my throat. The memories of growing up here, of existing on the cusp of something that the world around me insisted was desirable. But L.A. was confusingly ugly to me. Strip malls and expensive things you could look at but not touch.

It was just the two of us, my mother, Ava, and me, and no matter how often we moved apartments, we always lived on the edge of pretty things—at the uglier flat-bottom of famous hills stacked with beautiful homes; in the clothes other people donated, still soaked with their rosy perfume. I pretended to long for the same pretty things my mother wanted most: money, movie roles, someone to love her. But I had my own secret list: someone to watch over me and pick me up from school on time. Someone to tuck me into bed and still be there in the morning. Someone to ask me *what the hell were you thinking?* when I fucked up. I wanted to be grounded by a parent who expected great things of me. I glance at Emmy's little body next to mine. Her big eyes watching out the window. Maybe the way Lorraine Duncan digs her claws into parenting isn't so bad after all. Maybe it means someone to make you breakfast and drive you to school and to help you dispel the feeling that you will never be special enough to survive.

Unless, according to my mother, you are famous. Famous for *what* is less important.

As if reading my mind, Emmy asks, "Will we see Grandma?"

"Grandma is pretty busy these days."

"Doing what?"

Doing whatever she feels like.

The plane banks, circling the airport. "I wasn't going to tell you this, but the people I'm here to meet with gave us three tickets to Disneyland. Should we go?"

"Disneyland?" Emmy's eyes are as wide as her grin. "Yes!"

"You're using Disney already?" Oliver whispers. "Won't we need it as some kind of bribe later on?"

"I didn't plan on using it so soon."

"I'd like to see her too. Your mom."

"Mm-hmm. Oliver? Did you know we're going to Disneyland?"

"Won't work on me, sorry." He takes my hand and kisses my fingers. "You have to admit, if she's not your mom, she's kind of . . . fun? Maybe a quick dinner?"

"Maybe," I say to the sprawl outside the window.

I focus on our itinerary: a day at Disneyland; my meeting with Allison Kidd, Natalie's producing partner; the Dirty Diana party and a week at Petra's house in Malibu. The plane hits a bump and I flinch, squeezing my eyes shut. When they open, the universe serves me a pick-me-up: A woman, one row up and across from us, is scrolling the Dirty Diana site. I fight the impulse to take a picture and send it to Alicia.

Just before baggage claim, we're greeted by a chauffeur holding a lit-up sign that reads *Diana Wood*.

"That's you!" Emmy squeals.

Ernest has a mane of long white hair and forty years on us but doesn't allow us to carry a single bag. He loads our luggage onto a cart and zips us through the hidden shortcuts of LAX, out the door, and across six lanes of insane traffic. We follow like frogs from one lily pad to the next. In the parking lot, Emmy hops her tiny body into Ernest's black SUV and the back seat swallows her whole. She tucks her legs beneath her, transfixed by the big screen that plays trivia and the many tiny bottles of water and wrapped mints. "Are these for free?" she whispers.

"I think we've just made her whole trip," Oliver says, laughing as Emmy grabs a generous handful of candies.

On the way to the hotel, I can't get my mom out of my head. Against my better judgment, I text her.

We may be coming to LA!

Most likely she won't reply for weeks and then I'm sort of off the hook for not telling her at all? It's the kind of bad math that never works out and still I do it.

Ernest hears Emmy say she's hungry and takes us for burgers at In-N-Out. In the drive-through line, he calls, "Anyone like milkshakes?"

Emmy raises her hand.

"Gotta order the 'Around the World.' It's on the secret menu. Has all the flavors."

Oliver bites into his first Double-Double. "You're right. It's totally better here."

"When did I say that?"

"Even the milkshakes taste better than Texas," Emmy agrees.

"Ever been to L.A. before?" Ernest asks.

"It's been awhile," I say, happier to just be a tourist.

"You like city views?"

"Sure."

"Check out the observatory. It's in Griffith Park, near your hotel. Got views that will take your breath away. You like pie?"

Emmy raises her hand again. "I do!"

"Right by the observatory is a place called Trails. Great place for pies. What about fish? You like fish?"

Emmy scrunches up her nose and Ernest clarifies, "Not to eat. To look at."

"Oh." Her tiny shoulders relax. "Definitely."

"Make sure your parents take you to the aquarium in Long Beach. It's beautiful. You like waves, don't you?"

"I know how to surf. Sort of."

"Good for you. My favorite beach is right between Topanga and Santa Monica. Pier 26. You like Mexican food?"

"Yeah."

"So many good ones. I like El Compadre on Sunset but lots of good spots downtown."

Oliver leans close to me. "You like oxygen?"

"I like Ernest." I smile.

The studio has put us up at the Chateau Marmont in Hollywood. Growing up, I drove past it hundreds of times and imagined what it was like inside. From the outside, it's a small, weathered castle tucked into the hillside. A place for famous people to both be seen and to disappear. We pull in and spot our first celebrity—a muscular blond in sunglasses, reasonably tattooed, waiting for his car at valet.

As we enter the storied hotel with its original Spanish tile and Gothic touches, Oliver asks, "Isn't this where Belushi died?"

"Ernest would have known."

"You like tragedies?"

We drop our bags in our room and immediately zigzag through the hotel's maze of garden bungalows, dressed up in bougainvillea, on our way to the pool. It all feels so California. The striped umbrellas. The crispness in the air. Not an ounce of humidity. The honking from Sunset Boulevard just yards away. The smell of jasmine to balance it out.

Seventy-two degrees is a chilly day to Californians, but Emmy dives into the water without a thought. She orders chicken fingers poolside and Oliver and I drink mojitos from our lounge chairs. The only other poolgoer reclines on her chair, across the oval-shaped pool from us, reading *Vanity Fair*.

Oliver tilts his face up to the sun. "L.A. really sucks you in, doesn't it?"

"It's nice, right?"

"Why did you ever leave?"

"Watch this!" Emmy cannonballs into the pool for the fortieth time. Oliver and I cheer softly, careful not to disturb the *Vanity Fair* woman.

After dinner, we tuck Emmy into her rollaway cot, then sit out on our private patio out of her earshot. Our room is off the hotel's main building and from here, we have a view of the pool below and its orange loungers, palm trees, and a sliver of Sunset, all lit up and lined with billboards. We take a hit off the complimentary vape pen.

"Could this be our lives?" Oliver asks, then coughs on the weed.

I smile, taking in the cloudless sky, the way his shoulders have already relaxed.

"We're anonymous," he marvels. "We could do anything."

"People would eventually know us. Just like anywhere."

"Maybe. But maybe with fewer rules."

Neither one of us wants to go to bed. There's a slight breeze through the palm trees. Even the striped umbrellas give a gentle, romantic shrug in the wind. The tiled patio is cool beneath my feet. Maybe it's the weed but the air feels charged.

When I turn my face toward Oliver, he holds my gaze. He has a hungry look in his eyes, and my body instantly responds. I get up from my chair and hover above him. He takes my hand and pulls me closer until I'm in his lap, straddling his hips. The ocean is miles away but I swear I can smell the salt water. I kiss him and tell him how good he tastes. He sweeps the hair from my neck and kisses along my jaw down to my breasts, both of us making contented noises, small and quiet.

"Show me three things you like," he whispers into my neck.

"This." I take off my Longhorns T-shirt and let it fall to the ground. Oliver takes one of my nipples in his mouth and cups my other breast with his hand. I press into him, tightening my legs around his hips.

Oliver says, "Show me what else."

"This." I take his hand between my thighs, showing him just the right pressure and speed.

"Like this?" he says when I let go.

"Slower."

He responds. And I want to draw this out, stay out here forever. I lift my hips then stand, just long enough to slip my underwear off. I lower myself back into his lap and guide his fingers slowly back inside me, lining them up so they rub against my G-spot.

Oliver moans louder this time and I cover his mouth, both of us laughing. My head feels light and my whole body has invited the sensation of being stoned and somewhere new. "Show me one more thing you like," he says, into my hand.

"This." I unbutton his pants and together we pull them off, moving faster now, until he is naked too. I push farther into the chair. I feel the smooth skin of his erection before guiding him inside me.

"This is my favorite," I tell him, lifting my hips. We move together in languid circles. "My favorite," I repeat. Oliver's breath on my neck. The skin of his chest, taut and smooth, against my breasts. My favorite sensation is Oliver inside me. My favorite touch is his hand at the small of my back, holding me. My favorite reaction is his mouth, slack with pleasure.

Below us, two silhouettes swerve drunkenly to the pool and fall onto a single lounger. I place my lips on Oliver's to quiet the sound of his breathing. The others are nearby but oblivious. Just feet away.

We stop kissing, gasping for breath, Oliver leans back, then drops his chin in imitation of Ernest. "You like sex?"

"Yes."

"There's this guy you should meet. He's staying at the Chateau Marmont." Oliver begins to laugh, stoned and happy. I press my hand against his mouth again to muffle any sound. He gently bites at my palm and now we're both laughing. He buries his face in my chest and I hold him there to steady us both.

"We have to finish," I insist. "It feels too good."

A small smile still plays at the corner of his lips and I want to melt into him I'm so in love. His mouth opens slightly like he's going to say something else but he doesn't. We hold each other's gaze and all I want to do is stop time and live in this moment forever.

"Make me come," I whisper, and his smile slowly disappears. He nuzzles my neck and a delicious chill runs up my spine. I look up into the sky, palm trees swaying above us. I smell the salt air, then the chlorine on Oliver's skin. We are still stoned. We're bleached by the L.A. sun, languid and blissful as we fuck. Oliver moves in and out of me, faster and faster, until both of us are completely overcome. "Diana," he moans again and again. My fingers dig into him and this time he covers my mouth as I cry out in ecstasy.

On Saturday, we walk a few blocks in the California sunshine and wait in line for banana pancakes at The Griddle, which we all agree are worth it. We spend the rest of the day by the pool, still only a handful of other people around. We drink mojitos in the hotel's famous sunroom. We listen to guests at the table next to us discuss weekend box office totals. We're so in love with the Hollywood charm of the hotel we never want to leave.

We eat an early dinner in the room and watch *Vertigo* in bed, Emmy between us. She's asleep before James Stewart is hired to report on Kim Novak's strange behavior. Oliver reaches across Emmy to hold my hand and we fall asleep like this.

On Sunday, Emmy is wide awake and dressed by seven A.M. The concierge has provided us with a rental car and we're on our way to Disneyland by seven thirty. Even Emmy is confused by the heaviness of the Sunday traffic. "A lot of people must be going to church."

"L.A. is beginning to lose a bit of its charm," Oliver says, changing lanes.

An assistant in Natalie Hutton's production office sent instructions telling us to park at one of the Disney hotels and pick up our tickets there. But when we arrive, a woman dressed like Mary Poppins is standing near the desk holding a sign with my name on it.

"It's just like the airport!" Emmy marvels.

Mary Poppins explains that she's our private guide for the day, courtesy of Natalie's team. We smile politely, imagining a day of chatting about Disneyland's rich history until we realize that her real job is getting us to the front of every line. It's game-changing. As we skip to the front of the ninety-minute Space Mountain line, Oliver whispers, "How badly do they want your life rights?"

When we exit the ride, Emmy shouts, "Can we go again?" and we circle back to the front of the line. By the end of the day, Emmy is levitating, swinging a new light saber and carrying her princess autograph book full of big, looping signatures. She falls asleep two minutes into the ride home and Oliver carries her into the hotel room and gently lays her on the rollaway bed. I un-Velcro her sneakers and as Oliver pulls off her Elsa watch, Emmy opens her eyes and asks Oliver if we are going to all live together again.

"I hope so." He kisses her cheek and by the time he switches off the light, she's lightly snoring.

I swipe a bottle of rosé from the fridge, and Oliver and I head to the patio, as if this has been our nightly routine for years. Oliver takes a seat while I stand at the railing, both of us looking out over the pool. We recap our day, including our shared suspicion over whether our guide is sleeping with Goofy.

"She was so professional until he appeared," I remark. "Emmy didn't even ask for a picture and she practically dragged us over."

"I wonder what he looks like under the costume? He could be a young George Clooney?"

"But wouldn't Disney have made him a prince?"

For several minutes, we fall completely silent. I listen to the sound of cars from Sunset Boulevard below, laughter and clinking glasses from the pool. In the quiet, Oliver says, "There's something so lonely about single parenting. Did you ever feel it?"

I turn to face him. He looks as tired as I feel. "Every day."

"Not to say we should get back together because our days with Emmy will be easier but . . ."

"No, of course not."

"How is it going for you? Is that how I say it? How does a good communicator ask his girlfriend that is still his wife if she is happy?"

"Is that what you go by these days?" I tease. "A good communicator?"

"I guess if you have to ask—"

"I am. Happy. You?"

"Yes. But . . ." He steadies his glass on his knee, keeping his eyes on it and not on me. "As a good communicator . . . The truth is, there is this shadow for me. Of how things were before. I don't want to go back."

"Me neither."

"So what do we do?"

"Keep going." I move toward him. I set his glass on the table and climb into his lap. "Keep being honest with each other."

He wraps his arms around my waist and kisses my neck. "Keep touching each other."

"Yes."

"Even when we were apart, I still felt this connection to you. I hated it most of the time. That I couldn't get you out of my head."

"I want to stay in your head." I kiss his cheek, his stubble short and rough against my lips.

"Me too."

"Show me three things you like."

Chapter Twelve

The Sony Studios lot reminds me of a well-manicured college campus. Bright green lawns and narrow pathways winding through neatly arranged office buildings and art deco facades. Everywhere I turn, I see dozens of executives, heads in their phones, rushing to work. I struggle with my map, making my way past enormous soundstages and out of the way of honking golf carts.

The restaurant on the studio lot is packed. I arrive six minutes late, covered in a thin layer of sweat, from a mixture of nerves and rushing in the heat. At the host stand, a willowy woman smiles. Her teeth are just the right amount of crooked to be charming. I find myself mourning them—in the small moments it takes her to check my reservation and let me know "I have a table by the window for you," I've already pictured her landing an acting job, quitting the restaurant job, and scheduling an appointment for veneers.

"Thank you," I say and follow her to the empty table. The willowy woman hands me a menu and within seconds, a waiter named Tucker takes my order. His smile is jittery and his white shirt is clean but wrinkled. As Tucker sets down my iced tea, my eyes wander the room, taking in the yellow daisy centerpieces, the floor-to-ceiling windows that look out onto the perfectly manicured lawn. I gaze out onto the busy sidewalk watching two women say goodbye. Their embrace is quick and neat and when they break apart, I lose my breath. The space between them has opened wide enough to reveal a man, tall and broad shouldered, exactly like Jasper. He's far enough away to be blurred at the edges, but I can make out a familiar posture in the way he nods as he listens to a woman in a red-and-white-striped sundress. Is she an actress? A girlfriend? Is that really Jasper? It can't be. He's in London. Or Paris. Or New York? Not L.A.

I stand to get a better look but by the time I get close enough to the window, he's pressing his cheek to the woman's, then turning away. It all happens so quickly. The man who might be Jasper is there for a moment and then absorbed into the crowd, gone.

I drop back into my chair, relieved Allison Kidd isn't here yet to see my cheeks flush or my hands shake. Could it actually be him? And what if it is? Do I run after him? To say what—*just saying hello so we can have one more goodbye*? I bow my head and pretend to look for something in my purse so no one can see me closing my eyes and catching my breath. The familiar sharp urges are still there—the ones telling me to go after him for no other reason than to be near him for a few extra minutes—but so is the patio at the Chateau and Oliver's twinkling blue-green eyes. Allison enters the restaurant and Jasper leaves my mind—I send him away. Everyone has a doppelgänger. I must have discovered his.

I recognize Natalie's producing partner from my Google search—*Variety, The Hollywood Reporter, Deadline*—always the same two photos used in rotation: an outdated corporate headshot with a tight smile and arms crossed and a red carpet shot, Allison and Natalie in an embrace, Allison so petite that her entire frame tucks neatly into Natalie's. She's Ivy League all grown up, toned arms in a sleeveless black dress, and just the right amount of jewelry and confidence.

"Diana! You're real!" She gently squeezes my shoulders and sits. "Not that I doubted you were. But your voice from the interviews—I've been so lost in it, it's so otherworldly." She narrows her eyes and suddenly I can't decide if I'm a pleasant surprise or an alarming disappointment. "How's L.A.? How's the hotel?"

"It's gorgeous. Thank you so much."

"Ugh. We should have lunched there!" Her hands are in constant motion, a man's gold Rolex swinging from her tiny wrist. "I love the Chateau. I'm going to kill my assistant."

"This place is great too. I've never been on a real studio lot." This is a lie. As a kid, I spent long afternoons riding shotgun with my mom to auditions at studios all over L.A., trying to read a *Thomas Guide* and get us there safely. Then sitting in the car for hours while she was inside.

"Ha, yes. Isn't Hollywood beautiful? With all its bumper-to-bumper traffic?" She doesn't laugh at her own joke exactly but smiles wide enough to let me know that I should. "And how was Disneyland? You did the whole VIP thing?"

"We had the best day, thank you."

"It's the only way to do it. You'll never go back."

It's become a familiar, repeated sensation on this trip—the feeling of jumping the line. Sitting across from Allison, I worry I've missed a step. Someone is going to show up at the table and remind me I'm not supposed to be at this lunch. I'm supposed to be the assistant who in about forty-five minutes will be yelled at for picking the wrong restaurant.

"So. Natalie, who we all *love,* turned me onto Dirty Diana, which *I* now love, and *you,* who I know I'm *going* to love . . ."

"That's very kind."

"Honestly? I don't think I can make another bullet-train-fast-furious-dinosaur-explosion saga. Don't tell anyone I said that. I'd be fired."

For the next several minutes, Allison sprinkles candor onto everything she says with the intended effect of putting me at ease. It works—but more effective is the way she squints across the table at me when she talks, like she needs glasses but is in denial, and the way, when yet another executive stops by our table to say hello, her eyes go momentarily flat with exhaustion. I find it easy to picture her in an endless loop of pitch meetings and her mind somewhere else. When our salads arrive, she cuts to the chase.

"You seem like a no-bullshit kind of person."

"It's an aspiration."

"So I'm going to be very honest with you and if it scares you away, it scares you away."

"Okay," I say, already scared.

"We're going to offer you a decent amount of money for your life rights, which will then become our life rights. We will tell your story how we want to tell it. You will have very little impact on the storytelling. Likely all the ways we could make you happy about the script would be at odds with making a movie that succeeds, which will always be our number one priority. I just want to be up front so you know what you are getting into." She stops long enough to pick at the chicken in her salad. "It won't ever go the way you think it will. And it might not ever go at all."

"Got it," I say as if it all makes perfect sense.

"Any questions? About me? About the process?"

"Why would a person say yes to this?"

She smiles. "You're funny. Oh, well, your business will most likely explode, in a good way. You'll be a brand."

"And what's the brand that sells movie tickets?"

"Good questions and who knows? What sells today most likely

won't sell a year from now. The good thing is, sex always sells. And Nat, obviously. Her numbers are dependable."

"So I should what? Take the money and run?"

"No. You ask for a producer credit. Dammit. Don't tell anyone I said that either. Ha!" She reaches across the table and gives my hand a squeeze. "See? You get people to say what they shouldn't, even in this town. You're going to weather Hollywood just fine."

On the ride back to the hotel, I float into an alternate universe where my life is made into compelling storytelling then wonder about telling Oliver that I saw Jasper. Or that I think I saw Jasper. People think they see people every day. Is it even worth mentioning?

The traffic along La Cienega slows to a crawl. As if she can sense I'm near, my mother texts me.

> Are you here?

Of course she somehow knows I'm already in town. My body tenses. Information has always held power with my mom. A sure way to a fight is to hear something before she does and keep it to yourself. If a distant cousin graduates from high school and you don't immediately drop everything to tell her, it is a declaration of war. The joy of a former neighbor's new baby is immediately ignored if I've known longer than she has. There is no worse person to be than the last to know.

> I was actually about to text you. We made it!! Double exclamation points.

Her reply is swift. How long have you been here?

My lie is equally quick: Just landed.

> Were you going to tell me?

> Of course.

> I'd love to see my granddaughter. If that's all right with you.

My shoulders are nearly at my ears.

> Great. I'm sure she'd like that.

> I'm shooting all afternoon so why don't you bring her by set? She'll get a kick out of seeing me in my element.

I take a deep breath and hit the thumbs-up. There isn't anything I'd like to do less.

The film set is a dusty, flat piece of land near a series of small, desolate caves once used in the original *Batman* television show. Today it functions as a grad student film location, cheap and easy to secure. Oliver and Emmy follow me out of the rental car, each of us instantly mourning the loss of air-conditioning. "Here we are," I say, falsely chipper for Emmy. "This is it. Set." Camera equipment and sandbags are scattered around in the dirt in random lumps, and sunburnt actors sit on beach chairs they must have brought from home. Craft services is a card table with shriveled baby carrots and warm water bottles tucked behind a large rock. The crew all look like college students, and like the actors, they've wilted in the sun.

Memories of being on locations as a kid come flooding back. The waiting. The boredom. Parsing out trips to the craft service table for Hershey's kisses to pass the time. Making myself invisible when anyone important-looking passed by, worrying they'd fire my mom for bringing me to work.

"And there's your mom!" Oliver looks genuinely excited. I rest my hands on Emmy's shoulders and try my best to draft off Oliver's good mood.

My mother has hardly aged. She looks spry if maybe a bit overheated. Still easily the most beautiful woman onset with her golden-brown eyes and auburn hair, falling in easy curls to her shoulders.

"Diana! God, it's been too long. I barely recognize you." The dig is so slight it's almost imperceptible.

Her embrace is quick, then she turns to Oliver. "Just as handsome as ever." She makes a big show of hugging him close in front of the crew.

"What are you shooting?" he asks. "It looks like quite a production."

"No, not really. But I enjoy doing these student films. Supporting young artists. And they appreciate getting to work with a more seasoned actress like me. That's what we say, Oliver, *'seasoned'* . . . " She winks. She's one of the rare few who can get away with it.

"Well, it looks like a fun day's work."

"The director's got a ton to learn. He keeps flashing me a *V* symbol."

"What's that?"

"Exactly. *Vulnerable,* he tells me it means. He's an international director. From Canada, I think. And these young guns are so used to emojis and texting that they forget how to give simple, actionable direction. So I'm getting hand gestures. What am I supposed to do with *V*? Right, Emmy?"

For the first time, she acknowledges Emmy, who has been smiling up at her this entire time.

"Hello." Emmy holds out her hand.

"Manners! I love it." She kisses Emmy's hand like she's royalty. Emmy beams. "You look *exactly* like me when I was little. Does your mom ever tell you that?"

"No."

"I bet she doesn't," she says with a tight smile.

"You look great." I play nice. "Like the heat doesn't bother you one bit."

"I have to set an example, right? When the budget is scant, you only have the passion."

One of the stressed-out crew members waves in our direction.

"Emmy, you want to sit by the monitor? And see Nona Ava in action?"

As they walk away, my mom takes Emmy by the hand and stage-whispers, loud enough for me to hear, "I've been wanting to spend more time with you but your mother barely answers her phone."

When she leaves, I realize I've been holding my breath.

"Nona Ava?" Oliver asks. "Is she Italian now?"

"Anything to avoid 'Grandma.'"

We follow Ava to the monitor, where she coos to the director. "Derek, sweetheart. You don't mind if my friend Emmy sits next to you and watches my big scene, do you?"

"Fine. But we're running out of light, gotta move." He turns up the speed on his neck fan.

"Noted. Anything else you want from me? Anything different this time?"

"Run faster."

"That I can do. Where's makeup? Makeup girl? Last looks. That's what you should be saying, dear," she instructs the young brunette with a fanny pack full of brushes. "Next time you'll get an AD, Derek. Makes life so much easier."

The bored brunette dabs at my mom's forehead with some translucent powder, soaking up beads of sweat, then shuffles away.

"That's all I need?" Ava smiles. "I must look better than I thought!"

Emmy sits next to the monitor as Derek yells "Action!" over the whir of his fan.

On cue, my mom runs through the dark cave with admirable commitment, screaming as she looks over her shoulder and back again. But she's not fast enough—a masked man grabs hold of her waist, spins her toward him, and plunges a knife directly into her chest. Fake blood blooms across her shirt, then drips down her skinny arms.

Emmy's eyes widen, and Oliver takes her by the shoulders, shifting her small body toward the craft service table. "Are those M&Ms?" he asks, whisking her away.

Irritated mostly at myself, I watch my mom milk her death scene. The masked villain stabs her again, this time in the neck. Ava struggles for breath as the production assistant crouches behind a rock, pumping more blood into a tube. It shoots toward Ava's face in a thick spray. The effect is horrifying and sloppy. Liam would be disappointed in their craftsmanship.

Ava steals a glance at the camera that is zooming in on her frightened expression. Her big eyes go wider and wider then freeze. Derek seems unimpressed. He makes a small V with his fingers and holds it above the camera. Ava responds by letting out a few forced gasps before finally closing her eyes.

"Cut!" Derek shouts. "We got it!"

No one helps my mom up or offers to clean the sticky blood from her skin. By the time I reach her, she's on her feet, but limping. "Guys! You have to clear the set and make it safe for the actors. I didn't want to ruin the take, but I'm barefoot here. We talked about this. There are very sharp rocks on the ground." But no one is listening. The sound guy approaches her and strips off her mic.

She brushes her wavy bangs from her forehead, sticky with sweat and fake blood. "What did you think?"

"Are you okay?"

"Oh yeah. Just a few cuts and scrapes. I've learned to use the pain. It helps." She sits on a rock and dusts off her feet then slips into a pair of worn Ugg boots. "How about I get cleaned up and we can meet at Casa Vega like old times? You can meet my new beau."

"Oh." I notice the way her hand quivers as she brushes the dirt from her knees. She's thinner, too, than the last time I saw her. A little hollower beneath her eyes. "You have a new boyfriend?"

"He's a yogi. Very successful. And I know what you're thinking. *You hate stretching. You loathe exercise!*"

I'm thinking, *This man has something you want*. I'm thinking, *Thank god I live in Texas because you will blow this up in some catastrophic way and at least I won't then have to avoid him, just like all the ex-boyfriends and landlords and bosses we ran from.*

"I'm thinking how cool. Yoga."

"Where's my granddaughter?"

"It was a little too much for her."

"She's too sensitive." She smiles up at me, an insult wrapped in a compliment on the tip of her tongue . . . "Just like her mom."

The hotel babysitter is named Jazz. She has a head of yellow curls and happens to have voiced a llama on one of Emmy's favorite cartoons. As Oliver and I leave for dinner, Emmy consults with Jazz on her latest headshot. "I like the one where you're smiling."

"Yeah. That's my agent's favorite too. You don't think it looks too 'network'? You know what I mean?"

"Maybe. . . ." Emmy pretends to understand. "A little?"

On our way to the restaurant, I try to sound casual when I say to Oliver, "I think I saw Jasper today. On the Sony lot."

"Jasper, Jasper?"

"Mm-hmm." I throw in a nonchalant, "Maybe."

"Oh." Oliver keeps his eyes on the road. "You didn't say hi?"

"No. It was right before my meeting."

"But it might not have been him?"

"Probably not. What are the chances?"

"When did you talk to him last?"

"Not since . . . hmm . . ." I know exactly how long it's been since Jasper and I spoke. And where we were. It was in my bedroom. Tangled in each other's arms. "Not for a while."

"Did you want it to be him?" Oliver's brows furrow in confusion.

"I don't know? I would have said hi, of course. If I was sure it was him."

"Right."

"Yeah."

"Do you still think about him?"

"No. Not like that."

"But it didn't really end with Jasper. It's not like you two broke up."

"It ended." Like I hope this conversation is about to.

Oliver clears his throat. "If we weren't back together and you saw him, could there be a world where you picked up where you left off?"

"Oliver. It's over." I point to the brightly lit sign up on the right. "We're here."

Casa Vega is the restaurant my mom and I frequented the most, whenever we had something to celebrate. If it was a birthday, we'd dine on chips and salsa; she'd have a margarita and I'd order a Coke and we'd tell each other, *we're just here for the ambiance*. If she had just booked a part, we'd both order entrées. But we never, ever valet parked, no matter how flush Ava felt and no matter how far we had to walk. Valet parking was for losers who were missing out on the fresh air.

Oliver pulls up directly in front of the low-slung building, white with a red tiled roof. Without a thought, he hands the valet his keys. For a moment, a familiar chasm opens between us—Oliver has never walked eight blocks to avoid paying for valet parking or lived with a mom who makes you walk eight blocks because she's too embarrassed to let the valet guy inside her old car, with its permanent "check engine" light and mysterious rattle, the way it doesn't so much stop when you put it in park but shudder then die. There's a familiar, annoying ache in my chest—the part of me that sympathizes with my single mom and how hard it must have been on her, a softening of my armor that will remain until another of her tiny knives finds its way in.

Inside, our eyes adjust to the dim, romantic lighting, and I immediately spot Ava, ensconced in a red leather booth beneath a framed portrait of a triumphant bullfighter. Beside her a tall, skinny man in his early seventies with a remarkably thick head of gray hair takes a long pull off his beer. "This is Stevie," Ava says, beaming. They are planted in the middle of the booth and I'm relieved to take one of the two ends and not be trapped in the middle. Over our first round of drinks, Ava announces, "Diana and I did a few yoga retreats together. You remember those, Diana?"

"Me?" is all I can think to say.

"Yes, *you*. With DeeDee and Maria. I would drive you up the coast to . . . what's that town called . . . Bolinas!"

"Love Bolinas, man." Stevie whistles, low and soft. "Magical place."

"Very centering. Of course, Diana hated going. You'd cry the whole time. *Try new things*, I used to tell you, but you were such a homebody." Her first tiny knife skims but doesn't pierce my skin.

Oliver shifts the focus. "What do you do, Steve?"

"Call me Stevie, please. My dad was Steve."

Confusion flits across Oliver's face. "Right. Stevie."

"What don't I do? Main gig is I run a few yoga studios across L.A. Side hustle, I grow cannabis."

"Oh. Is that how you two met?"

Ava shoots me an annoyed, warning glance. "To be honest, I take yoga at a competitor's studio in Silverlake, near my place, but *of course* now I'm thinking about making a switch for Stevie. His studios are the best in L.A."

"We put in the work. And we grow everything on my property. From strawberries to romaine to marijuana."

"You should see this property! It's beyond. Reminds me of a huge-scale version of that little garden we had. You remember?"

"No." I feel myself descend into petulance. We never had a yard, let alone a garden, and for some unknowable reason this is the piece of revisionist history that is a bridge too far.

"Oh well. You were so little."

"What's life like in Texas?" Stevie asks.

"They have a beautiful home," Ava chimes in. "Just gorgeous. Two stories with the sweetest picture window. You could spend hours gazing out that window."

Oliver catches my eye: *She remembers our house?*

And she's being nice about it? I silently warn him, *Watch out.*

"It's perfect for families," Ava goes on. "Emmy must have a dozen friends right on her street."

She gives my hand a gentle squeeze. And now, once again, I'm at the top of a ski hill, trying to pick a route. But they're all treacherous, too steep and icy. If I choose to remain vigilant, sit rod-straight in this booth and mostly quiet through dinner, this will confirm Ava's case that I'm coldhearted and stuck-up. But at least I'd be steeling myself for her next move. Or I can exhale. Let my shoulders relax and remind myself that we are both grown-ups, trying in our own ways.

"Thanks, Mom. Emmy loves it."

Ava takes a sip from the salted rim of her drink, then dabs at her mouth with a napkin. "And you, honey? You still *number crunching*?" She scrunches her nose like Stevie has just farted.

"Nope." Oliver jumps in, thinking he's helping me out. "She quit!"

"You quit your job?" Ava's hand covers her mouth dramatically as if I've also kept from her that I'm dying and have won a Nobel.

"I did, yep."

"Wow." She masquerades her anger with surprise. Here she is, *the last to know*. "To become what, honey? A math teacher?"

Only Ava could successfully fling this as an insult.

"I've started painting again." This feels nonthreatening enough. I'm not competition for her and I can already see her mind racing, flooded with an image of me selling my wares on a foldout table at an amateur art show where I'm largely ignored.

"Painting. Really." She lays a hand on Oliver's shoulder. "You certainly are a gem of a guy. Keeping it all afloat."

"Actually, Diana has a bigger paycheck than I do." I wish I were sitting closer so I could nudge him under the table.

"Maybe," I cut in. "But not by much. Oliver is flipping houses! Did you know that?"

"No one cares about my remodels when you're about to be in *Vogue*."

"*Vogue*?" My mother's voice is tight and high.

"I've been interviewing women who want to share their erotic fantasies, for a website I've created. It's a project I started in Santa Fe and picked back up." I catch an imagined glimpse of myself in her eyes. Only the top of my head is visible as if I'm being swallowed by the leather booth. "Kind of a side project."

Ava's expression goes stony. I watch to see if she'll blink.

"We're here talking to a studio about movie rights." If Oliver has picked up on anything, he doesn't let on.

"Wonderful!" Stevie exclaims. "The apple doesn't fall far from the tree."

"Movie rights to what exactly?"

"We're in the exploratory phase," I say. "Figuring out the story." Less is more.

"But they're not your fantasies? On the website?"

"No."

"And now someone wants to make a movie about a website?" She emphasizes the word *website* as if it's a wholly foreign concept.

"We'll see." My mind races for a way to change the subject, but Ava's gaze has always had this same unnerving effect on me.

"I'm just surprised, that's all. You were such a prude as a kid." Here it comes. The knives get sharper.

"Where can we listen?" Stevie asks.

"On her website," Oliver pipes in; I know he's trying to help, but I can feel the heat rise to my cheeks and the word *website* feels more and more absurd every time someone says it—like we're playing a game where everyone takes a shot of tequila whenever someone says "website." "You have to see her paintings."

"Love to," Stevie says enthusiastically. "Your mother didn't tell me you were an artist."

Cue my mother. "Well, that's because her mother didn't know!"

"Well. Surprise," I say softly.

"Hmm," Ava says and the table goes quiet. Finally, even Oliver has acknowledged the tension and can't politely fix it. We crunch on chips and salsa for over a minute before my mother finally breaks the awkward silence. "Maybe I just don't get it. I go on the Bank of America website every day, but I would never make it into a movie!"

Stevie's face falls. She's gone too far, even for her. Her autocorrect blinks on immediately. "I mean. I'm probably missing something. I guess I've never understood your art."

At the valet stand, Stevie and Oliver hand over their tickets and pretend to admire a cherry-red Ferrari.

Ava is quiet. She's waiting for me to come to her.

"Well. This has been great," I say flatly.

"Very nice."

"You okay?"

Ava sniffs. "I'm just a little hurt. This is my business, you know. I sacrificed a lot so you could grow up in L.A. and I have to hear about your new career over tacos. I was the one who planted the seed."

"You did. Thank you so much."

"Don't patronize me. I could have helped you. You could have come to me."

"For what?"

Ava rolls her eyes and pulls her sweater closed. "I know the entertainment world better than you do! You clearly have no respect for me. If you did, you would have reached out."

"You're forgetting that we don't talk! You don't call me. It's what we do."

"Right. You don't need anything from me. No need to put a finer point on it."

She will always be better at this than me—fighting without fighting—she'll stay calm while I try to push away the red-hot temper of twelve-year-old me.

I take a deep breath and exhale. "Thanks for coming out, Mom. Emmy loves ballet and art and she plays soccer but doesn't like it."

Ava snorts. "Please don't make me out to be the bad guy, Diana. I'm *so sorry* that I grew up in a time when we couldn't talk about our vaginas for a living. I had to survive on my own. I didn't have a single person in my corner to help raise you."

"You're right. But thankfully you're in a good place. Acting jobs. And Stevie seems mostly normal. Go do yoga even though you hate it and you can't even touch your toes." It's low and silly and if my own anger weren't knocking me so off-kilter, I would have stooped even lower.

"My friends can't believe how poorly you treat me."

"You know, it's dangerous. To always change who you are to be with people. It's a dangerous message."

"To *whom*?"

"Me?"

She throws back her head and laughs like I've told the funniest joke of the evening, only barely a "ha" escapes her. "It's called survival, dear. And every woman does it. Isn't that what your whole project is about? Women pretending to be someone they're not?"

Stevie's shiny black Lincoln pulls up and he opens the door for her. Ava kisses Oliver on the cheek then fixes her eyes on me and smiles, too brightly. "Thank you for dinner." She gives me a brisk hug, says "I hope we can do this again soon," then disappears into the passenger seat of Stevie's car.

Watching her pull away, my jaw relaxes. The air comes back to my lungs. I play a game I haven't played in thirty years and whisper to myself. *Brilliant.Whatawonderfulidea.Youhavealwaysbeensobraveso creative.HowcanIhelp?Iamjustsoproudofyou.*

Oliver slips his arm around my waist. "You okay?" he asks softly.

"Yeah. Same old script."

"Still." Our rental car pulls up to the curb. "L.A. is definitely losing some of its charm."

There is a haunted apartment complex on Wilshire that I visited when I first moved to L.A. The rent was astronomical but I pretended I could afford it just to see the apartment where Charlie Chaplin once lived. The new manager was showing me the available units and told me that the previous manager, who lived there for like thirty years, would sneak into the penthouse after dark, stay there for a few hours, and leave looking totally disheveled. Turns out a spirit was visiting him every night and they were fucking. It became their ritual. She was horrified but I was intrigued. I don't know if I'd have the nerve to do it, but in my fantasy I'd sneak into that same penthouse, lie on the bed in my skimpiest lingerie, and see what happens.

Chapter Thirteen

In the morning, we pack our suitcases, scrambling to find Emmy's missing sandal and squeezing the water from her still-wet bathing suit. Emmy sits on my suitcase so I can zip it closed and then runs for the elevator. Oliver and I check for chargers and forgotten toothbrushes, and with one last satisfied survey of the room he says, "I'll miss quiet patio sex."

On the drive to Petra's, we take turns guessing what her house looks like. Emmy decides it'll look like a cross between her two favorite rides, Splash Mountain and Cinderella's Castle. She's not totally wrong.

Behind the gates of Malibu Colony, we follow a long, winding driveway bringing us closer to the shore, to Petra's front door.

"This can't be it." Oliver's eyes go as wide and sparkly as the ocean.

Petra's housekeeper, tall and trim with a sleek blond ponytail, greets us at the front door. "I'm Brina." She grabs three bags at a time. "Anything you need just let me know."

"I *definitely* want to live here." Emmy sighs then runs through the wide-open living room straight for the deck, and down the wooden stairs leading directly to the sand.

"Bathing suit first! Sunscreen!" I turn in a full circle, trying to remember which suitcase has what.

"I'm happy to take her for a swim," Brina offers.

"Really?"

"Sure. Take your time and settle in. We'll be just out front; first I'll take Emmy's bag back and get her into her suit."

After Brina calls Emmy to come up and change, Oliver and I step onto the deck set high on stilts dug into the beach. The waves are small and calm today, gently rippling onto the shore. Soon we see Brina and Emmy chasing the tide, following it as it recedes and then giggling as it hits their ankles and splashes their knees. "This house is unreal," Oliver tells me, "but Brina is the best part of L.A."

"Emmy is not going to want to leave for her grandparents'."

The waves are too small to bodysurf but Emmy tries anyway, hurling her small body forward and then scrambling for the shore. She tumbles into the sand then pops back up and runs for the next. Again and again.

"She's not coming inside any time soon. Come on, I have something to show you."

I follow Oliver into the house. He reaches for his bag and digs around, then pulls out a shiny silver pair of handcuffs. His eyes crinkle in the corners the way they do when he's hoping I'm as genuinely excited as he is. This expression used to get under my skin, like he was pressuring me to be happy about the same things he was, in the exact same moments. But here, in Petra's living room with its vaulted ceiling and the sun streaming in, it feels less like a demand or even a plea and more like . . . an invitation.

His smile, too, is infectious.

"When did you have time to get those?"

"You can get anything in L.A. I also found—"

"They have an outdoor shower!" Emmy calls from the beach.

Oliver quickly tucks the handcuffs back in his bag. From the deck, we watch Emmy play in the surf until someone else on Petra's house staff, a lanky man in a crisp white polo shirt, approaches me with fresh celery juice and a cell phone.

"I have Petra for you."

On the other end of the line, Petra tells me she wants to be on the phone when I see the room for me and Oliver. "Down the hall to your left, past the Nan Goldin."

I follow her directions to one of the guest suites, a sprawling room with walls painted a pale green, all the furniture a dark maple wood.

"It's gorgeous."

"Mitch called it the 'mint chip' room. But he secretly loved it."

The glass doors to the room lead out onto the deck, and down to the beach. They're open a crack now so I can hear the crashing waves. And in front of the sliding glass doors is a blank canvas set up on an easel, with another stack of canvases leaning against the wall. They bring a rush of excitement. Like holding a new book, all potential and adventure.

"You set this up for me?"

"Brina did. Which is essentially me."

Alicia is the next to arrive, an hour later, as floored by the place as we are. "Malibu. Jesus. What is happening right now?"

From behind her legs, I see Elvis's head of curls peeking out. I kneel to give his chubby hand a fist bump. Alicia's husband, Nico, lifts me off my feet in a bear hug. As I give them the tour, Elvis does not let his mom out of his sight. Wherever Alicia goes, Elvis is there, a small but determined shadow.

Twice, Nico tries to lure him away, first to see his room, then to the beach, but both times he shakes his head. "He's going through a little bit of a Mommy stage," Alicia tells me. "Which is weird, we can all acknowledge, because Nico is way more fun."

Nico sighs. "True."

At dinner, Elvis warms up to Emmy, but he still trails Alicia to the kitchen, the bathroom, the couch. Over ice cream, the six of us play UNO on the deck, the waves crashing in the dark behind us. The night is cool, and we bundle under the blankets and let Elvis win the last round. Emmy winks at me, more delighted to be in on the adult plan than to win herself. She follows Alicia to their bedroom and reads Elvis a story, the novelty of having a younger sibling coursing through her veins like sugar. Eventually, Oliver carries her off to bed, and a full hour later, Alicia finds me on the deck, everyone else already fast asleep.

"Oliver passed out putting Emmy to bed," I say.

Alicia scoots in next to me on the chaise and yawns an entire sentence, "I get it. I'm so tired I think I'm beyond sleep. It's a new state of being that's unpleasant and useless."

"Where's Nico?"

"Also beyond tired and watching monster truck videos to fall asleep. He says it works."

For a long time, we talk about how stunning Petra's house is.

"Do you think Petra ever gets lonely here?" I wonder. "It's so big."

"I would crush this house alone. Just thinking about it . . ." She trails off.

"We all need a vacation," I say not so helpfully.

"When does the independent part kick in?"

"Well, you see Emmy. It's all in stages . . ."

"But Elvis is not like Emmy. Elvis watches me when I go to the bathroom. And I have to watch him. Eye contact and everything. If I even turn away for a second, he gets scared."

"He loves you."

"And he loves his dad just as much, but somehow Nico gets a pass with him. He can come and go, no tears, no questions, just happy to see him when he comes home."

"It will get better."

"That's the thing. It's already great. But it hasn't gotten better. And so maybe it's me that can't keep up? You want to hear my fantasy?"

"Can I record it?" I tease.

"Of course. I'm serious. Hand me your phone."

Alicia rests the phone on her stomach and hits record. The waves crash and a car honks on the PCH. I smile thinking this is how we always did it before Petra invested in Dirty Diana and we had an actual soundproofed studio.

"I'm tired all the time. And I have no idea why because it feels like I don't even do anything. So last week I made a list of everything I did in a day. Starting from when I woke up and gave the dog her arthritis medicine to the end of the day when I crashed after putting Elvis to bed. And the list was dismal. It was full of things like Trader Joe's and calling the sanitation department to get new trash cans because ours have cracks in the bottom and rotten milk spills onto our sidewalks. I read fifteen mediocre scripts from my students and met with two undergrads to discuss their half-baked ideas and one of them cried even while I worried I was being way too easy on him. I cooked, got the car washed, and did three loads of laundry. Do you know how many pieces of Elvis's little clothes can fit in one load? Five hundred. I swear. Forever folding tiny pairs of shorts and marrying little pairs of mismatched socks the size of a lollipop. I fed shredded kale to our bearded dragon, who honestly eats better than I do, and who I secretly hope dies while I'm here because his care routine is insane, and I switched insurance plans to cover Nico's ADHD medicine, which took almost two hours and I said "representative" into the phone so many times I actually turned into a robot. I walked our dogs, cleaned up their poop from the backyard, and found old Chinese food that was making our fridge stink. That one I was proud of. It was really foul. And then I looked at the list and I thought, what the hell did I do today?"

"You're taking care of a lot of people."

"So are most people. But some days I'm so depleted at night and when I get into bed Nico gives me this look—this look I used to love and now I just want to slap him when I see it. And I don't really mean that about the bearded dragon. I'm actually very attached." She turns to me, a faint smile on her lips. "And if I had to tell you my fantasy right now it would be flying to Alaska. A truly remote part where no one lives. Not even that crazy lady."

"Sarah Palin?"

"Away from her. All by myself in a tiny cabin. Dressed warmly, of course, with a little fireplace. And no one for miles. No one to ask me for anything. Just silence. In the morning, I open the front door and it's sunny and so bright and covered in snow. And the air is so cold and the only sign of human life is my breath. In and out. The only sound is the crunch of my boots in the snow. But when I stop moving, so does the sound. And it's quiet again. Days and days of pure, absolute silence."

In the morning, we wake to the sound of diesel engines pulling up to Petra's front door. Four box trucks filled with catering supplies, chairs, and tables are swiftly unloaded for tomorrow's event. My heart immediately starts to race with nerves and excitement.

Oliver watches from the window. "How big is this party?"

"Petra doesn't do anything small. Even Mitch was massive. That's her joke, not mine."

Before I can argue we might get in the way, Oliver is out the door and helping carry everything inside. I throw on my sneakers, and on my way out the door smack into Liam and Kirby.

"Holy shit." Liam tosses his frayed duffel bag to the floor and I'm just happy L'Wren isn't here yet to see him do it. "Are we on *Love Island*?"

"Liam, please." Kirby picks up his bag and hands it back to him. They look as mismatched as ever, a set of polished silver on a paper plate.

"You're right. It's classier. Maybe *Bachelor in Paradise*."

"Are we allowed to talk about work?" Kirby asks me hopefully.

"Now? Sure . . ."

"Great. I worked out the sound design for Effie, Megan, and Vic's interviews. They're in your inbox. Happy to jump in—"

"Maybe we shouldn't talk about work," I say, looking out at the picturesque ocean view.

Kirby nods while Liam grins. "Isn't she the best?"

We spend the rest of the afternoon at the beach. I already miss Emmy, who's just left with Oliver for his parents' house in Montecito. Liam and Kirby help Elvis build a sandcastle while Alicia, Nico, and I make friends with the neighbors, a bohemian couple who worked in the aging and dyeing of costumes for movies and have lived in Malibu since the '70s. All the leather jackets in *Easy Rider* were aged by them, using rubbing alcohol, dirt, and oil. They take us on a walk down the beach and point out where Johnny Carson used to live and which houses were washed into the ocean when and then rebuilt. I look at the stilts holding up the homes and think about the nights the tide reaches that far up and what it must feel like to lie in bed in a thunderstorm and if you can feel the water as it crashes into those stilts like the spindly legs of a storybook witch.

Elvis and Nico chase each other up and down the beach until Elvis passes out in his mom's arms, and I tuck them both in under a towel beneath an umbrella. Kirby and Liam dip their toes in the water and decide they both prefer the Gulf, then immediately head back inside with their bedroom door locked.

Inside, I find Petra fresh off the plane. Suddenly the house feels right, like the missing piece has finally settled in. When I hug her, she's thinner than I remember, delicate beneath her long summer dress.

"What do you think?" She smiles.

"It's unreal." Together, we tour the house. Already gorgeous, every inch has been buffed, polished, and dressed up for tomorrow's party. The bars, indoors and out, are fully stocked, lined with menus of cocktails named after our interviewees. Dirty Diana gift bags have been arranged on a table near the door, our branding suddenly everywhere, ready for a guest list full of names I've only seen in tabloids.

I start to tell Petra how nervous I am to impress Vibezz, but she interrupts me. "Don't be nervous. Be excited."

Once she's satisfied with the setup, I ask if she'd like to take a walk on the beach. She says yes, then hesitates. She yawns and showily stretches her arms overhead. "I think I need a quick nap."

In the guest room, I curl up with my sketch pad and pencils. I try to capture the view outside the window, then the striped loungers by the hotel pool, then find myself absentmindedly sketching a '70s leather jacket.

I take a hot shower and when I get out, Oliver is here, changing from his shorts into jeans, his body still warm from the sun; I wrap my arms around him from behind and whisper in his ear. "Where are the handcuffs?"

He turns and smiles. He slips my robe off my shoulder and kisses my bare skin. "Don't we have to go to dinner?"

That night, Petra secures us an outside table at Nobu so we can admire the sunset as we eat. Petra sits across from me, looking rested but quieter than usual. As if picking up on her sadness, Oliver sits by her side and entertains her with our L.A. adventures. When he gets to Ernest, I hear her warm, gentle laugh, and my shoulders relax. The server fills my wineglass with a second, generous pour, and my head feels light and dreamy.

Alicia is deep in conversation with Liam after Nico convinced her to come out with us on her own and leave him and Elvis at home. Three drinks in, Kirby, who has been quiet the entire evening, whispers in my ear. "I'd like to do a fantasy."

"Really?"

"It feels a little hypocritical, right? Recording other women being vulnerable but never sharing anything about myself?"

I think of the *Vogue* Q&A, an unfinished copy still crumpled at the bottom of my purse. *What's your fantasy?* "Not necessarily."

"Liam and I talked about it and I want to try it."

As quickly as she announces this, she's up from the table, snapping pictures of the ocean from the patio's edge.

Liam watches her, smiling.

"How are you two doing?" I ask, though the way he smiles makes it obvious.

"Don't fish, D. This trip is perfect."

"I'm not fishing. We can talk about whatever you like."

"Great. Let's try adding a video element. We have the paintings and now we need the next piece."

"Are the wedding plans still on track?"

He rolls his eyes, but the soft creases of his eyes let me know he's not upset. "I know it feels rushed. But it also feels really right. Just like video feels really right for the company."

"It always feels right in the beginning," I warn.

"No more drinks for you."

"I like you both so much—"

"Then stop obsessing over our marriage." He looks down into his lap, adjusting his napkin. "You're not exactly an expert."

At that exact moment, someone passes behind Liam. He sweeps past, then stops, coming back into frame. A fully fleshed figure—tall, dark hair, and familiar dimples.

"Diana." Jasper's brown eyes look almost amber in this light.

"Jasper?" My heart pounds. "Hi."

"You're in L.A."

I hold his gaze too long. Under the table, Liam presses his foot into mine.

"Yes, for a couple weeks. What are you doing here?"

"A campaign poster for a tornado movie. It's an incredible film."

"Is it?"

"No, it's unwatchable but the job is fun." He laughs, his familiar dazzling smile on display. By now, he has the attention of the full table. I can feel their eyes on him, passing from him to me and back again. My face burns and I wish the sun had fully set so I could hide out. And that my head was less fuzzy with wine. All eyes are on him, but he's still looking only at me. "It's nice to be on autopilot and not have to think for a minute."

This time Liam doesn't gently nudge my foot but kicks me in the ankle.

"Jasper, this is Liam. And Oliver. And my friends, Petra and Kirby. Of course you know Alicia."

Jasper regards Oliver, a nearly imperceptible smile on his face. "Oliver. So nice to meet you."

"You too." Oliver returns Jasper's gaze and they lock eyes like friendly competitors shaking hands before a match. They seem to share a secret—it's me, and I'm sitting right here. I'm about to cut in when Jasper breaks the spell and makes his way around the table, shaking hands, kissing Alicia on both cheeks.

And then, back to me. He's standing behind my chair now. I scoot it out and it scrapes loudly against the wooden deck. I stand with my back to the table, everyone's eyes burning a hole through the back of my pink sundress. Alicia tries her best to refocus the table's attention on her by remarking too brightly, "These waves. Does the tide usually get so high? Ha. I sound like Blondie."

"I don't want to interrupt your dinner . . . and I have a friend at the bar. It's great to run into you," Jasper says. He gives me a quick hug.

"You too. Of course."

Petra, who refuses to pretend not to be listening, asks, "Are you in town for long?"

"Through next week."

And then it's Oliver who chimes in. "You should come to our Fourth of July party tomorrow. We're celebrating Dirty Diana."

"Yeah?" Jasper sounds as surprised as I am.

"Why not?" Oliver turns to Petra, who smiles as she says, "Why not?"

"Okay. I might do that."

When Jasper leaves, the table falls silent. Alicia turns to me. "I have to pee. You?"

"Sure."

"What was that?" she hisses once we're in the bathroom. "Seriously? I didn't know if he and Oliver were going to fight or kiss!"

"It was fine."

"And then Oliver invites him to the party? Like, *what*?"

"That part wasn't great."

"Are you freaking out? You must be freaking out."

"I'm fine." I wash my hands for the third time.

"Are you confused? Are you regretting anything? How are you feeling?"

There's only a tightness in my throat like I might run out of oxygen in the Nobu bathroom. "Surprised, that's all. And if we stay in here any longer, Oliver will worry."

As we make our way to the table she whispers, "Jasper didn't look that good, really. I don't like him with a tan."

"Of course. Everyone looks worse with a tan."

"What do you think Oliver is thinking?"

...

At the table, Oliver had seemed unfazed but back at Petra's, as we stand at the sink, brushing our teeth before bed, he says, "I didn't realize he was that good-looking."

I make the most neutral sound I can. "Mmm."

"He's very handsome."

"Yeah." I meet his gaze in the mirror and shrug. "I guess I've just known him for so long."

"It's okay to admit, Diana. He's universally beautiful." I reach for his shoulder, but he turns away from me to fill his water glass instead. "I get the appeal."

"Can we talk about something else?"

"What do you mean?" he asks.

"I mean like not obsess over Jasper's appearance."

"I'm not obsessed. Are you obsessed?"

"Oliver. No. I'm not."

"You sure?"

My jaw tenses. As if I purposefully brought Jasper to L.A. and this is somehow my fault? "It was never about his looks anyway."

"Right. He's naturally got a great personality. You already told me he was good in bed."

"What are we talking about right now? Are we fighting about this?"

"No." He's never sounded less convincing. "It's just, Katherine is beautiful too. But also someone you could imagine running into at the grocery store."

"I can imagine running into Jasper at the store. I have. It's not that shocking."

"Yes, but how would you feel if you bumped into me and Cindy Crawford was on my arm?"

"He wasn't on my arm tonight. I was sitting with you. I didn't even know he was in L.A."

I climb into bed and he follows.

"Have you two been talking?"

"You're blowing this completely out of proportion."

"I'm not. I know you want me to be this totally secure, new man but I can still be upended."

"That's not what I want."

"I'm different. We both are. And you don't want the old me."

"*You* don't want the old you! You were miserable. And I'm not here because you feel more confident."

"You lit up when you saw him."

"I was surprised. I get upended too." I won't lie to him. "You're right. He's that kind of guy. He just is. I'm sure everyone at the table wanted to fuck him."

"So you admit it?"

"Jesus, Oliver. Why did you invite him to the party?"

Oliver sits up in bed and runs his hands through his hair. "This is too much. There's too much pressure."

"What does that mean?"

"I don't know. I need to feel like I can have room to be ugly."

"Then you're off to a good start."

"Seriously?" he says, but it echoes through the room more like *Fuck you.*

I want to storm off but there's a house full of people and I don't know where to go. I get out of bed and step out onto our patio, inhaling the cool, salty air. Fighting is good. We're talking about our feelings. *Don't walk away. This is healthy.* Of course he's rattled. We'll take a few moments to ourselves, apologize, and move on. I relax when I hear Oliver get out of bed—but he doesn't join me. Instead the bathroom door closes with a slam. Was it louder than usual? Angrier? *He'll come back. Any second, he'll come out here. We'll tell each other it was a passing moment. We both care. That's all this is.* But when the bathroom door opens, Oliver doesn't join me. He turns off the bedroom light and I hear him settle onto the bed. I'm taken right back to the suffocating space we used to live in after fighting. There was no coming to find each other. We both groped for more space between us, not less.

Back in the room, even in the dark, I can feel Oliver's agitation.

"I'm taking a shower," I announce to his back.

Under the warm water, I close my eyes and breathe. The water runs hot, turns my skin pink, and the shower doors fog up.

I hear him before I can see him through the steam. I take a step back, inviting him under the water. He silently complies then pulls me to him so we're both getting wet. He lifts my arms over my head and lightly traces his fingers up my torso.

He presses me up against the tiles and parts my legs with his knee. I try to close them again, teasing him in resistance. But there is no foreplay. No tender kisses up and down my thigh. He knows what he wants. He kneels on the shower floor before me. When he looks up, his eyes are repentant, his lashes beaded with water. "I'm sorry for tonight. The whole night," he says.

I don't answer. His hands slip to my buttocks. He squeezes tight and buries his head between my legs. His mouth is on me, his lips wet and soft. His tongue, deep inside me. Every sensation is heightened, the tension of our fight still coursing through me. I reach for him, trying to pull him to stand, but he bats me away. "No," he tells me. "Just you." Oliver licks me long and slow, and when I shiver he takes me by the hips and moves me closer to the warm water. I bury my hands in his hair. My edge is so close that I want to slam on the brakes. Live in this moment where Oliver devours me for a little longer.

Oliver lifts his head and kisses my thighs, my hips, my stomach. I can't take much more. I grip his shoulders. "Please. I need you inside me. Now."

He stands, his gaze level with mine. He kisses me, the water running into our mouths. I lean against the wall and nearly slip before Oliver catches me. He presses his weight into mine. My breathing is ragged, my head light and floaty.

"I'm sorry too," I tell him.

After our shower, we climb into bed. My legs are still shaky with pleasure. Oliver falls quickly and soundly asleep.

But I am wide awake. Eventually, I give up on sleep and quietly make my way to the deck. I slide the doors shut behind me and take in the predawn light. The sky is a moody blue, just beginning to lighten. On the beach below, I see Petra, her back to me, sitting on a striped blanket near the shore.

"It's so early."

"Jet lag."

I sit beside Petra and she tucks the blanket over my legs.

"You smell like sex."

"I showered!"

"It's a vibe," she teases.

"Maybe I should have my picture taken. 'Sitting on the beach, just got fucked . . .'"

Petra laughs, but it's shallower than usual, her eyes fixed on the horizon.

"You all right?"

"I haven't been to the Malibu house since Mitch died."

"Oh. Petra." I turn to face her. She watches the tide and bites at her bottom lip, trying and failing to keep her eyes from filling with tears.

"I thought it would be easier if I had more people here, a house full. Mitch and I had so many happy times here. I thought maybe I'd feel some of that. Like happiness would be stored here and I could drink from it." She laughs and presses her palms against her eyes. "Like some stupid fountain." She takes a deep breath, but it catches in her throat, shaky and misbehaving. "I even brought some of his ashes. Just in case I wanted to scatter them in the ocean. . . . Don't worry, I'm thinking it too. So fucking cliché, I know." I notice it now, a plastic bag in the sand near her feet.

"It's not. I wasn't." I pull the sleeve of my sweatshirt down over my hand and brush the tears from her cheeks.

"It feels like he's going to walk through the door any minute. I actually froze this afternoon when I heard a truck pull into the driveway."

"It won't always be like this. This new."

"That's sad too." Petra rests her head on my shoulder. "Tell me something good."

My mind races and my thoughts are vapor. The sky is good, brightening. It looks like it'll be a nice clear day. "Something good. I get to be here with you."

"Hmm." Like *try again*.

"I'm excited about the party. I'm not nervous anymore."

"Something true, Diana."

"Weirdly I like you even more this morning than yesterday."

"Because I cried."

"Because you are the richest person I know and yet your husband's ashes are in a Ziploc baggie and not an urn made of gold and rubies and I find that strangely comforting."

She laughs. "Okay, that's good. Of course, full disclosure, Brina went out and bought us six different urns. They're inside and I hate them all even though they are objectively very beautiful."

"And made of rubies and solid gold?"

"Yes, that too." She settles back into me. The sky is now a pale blue tinged with orange. Soon the rest of the house will be awake. "I miss his arms. They were massive and so strong and when he held me, I felt like nothing could hurt me. It was like he was made of some other material than the rest of us get, something sturdier. Rock, but not cold—still warm and unpredictable like the rest of us. But you couldn't knock him over. Nothing would shock him or scare him away." She laughs, a tiny bit sheepish. "Even me."

She pulls her knees to her chest. "I don't like it here without him. I want to do all of it less. Sometimes I hate the rhythm of a day. When there's too much quiet I get scared to be alone and when there's too much noise I'm angry he's not part of it. And I don't have anyone to tell how shitty I feel at the end of the day. I just pretend all day long. But at least with Mitch, I had someone to tell that I felt like a fraud or I felt ugly or nervous. Or scared."

"You can tell me."

"Okay." Petra turns to me, her eyes glistening and worried. "I'm scared I won't survive this. That my grief is bottomless and I'll just keep falling."

I pull her into me and her shoulders shudder, crying into my chest. After a few minutes, she pulls away and wipes her eyes on the blanket.

"Maybe we scatter the ashes this afternoon," I say. "At the party."

"No. The party is going to be a scene. Just wait."

"What about now?"

"It's not too depressing? Just the two of us?"

"I don't think so. Or maybe just you? I didn't know Mitch."

She seems to consider the idea, watching the low tide come steadily nearer. "Maybe later." She tucks the bag into her lap. "He would have liked you."

"Yeah?"

"He would have ribbed you a little, of course. 'Jump in, Diana! Just fucking jump in!' That's what he used to say all the time. Feet first. Jump in. For everything."

Petra brushes the sand from her hands, then the blanket, busying herself to keep from crying again. When she's satisfied everything is tidy enough, she lies back on the blanket, one arm tucked behind her head and the other draped across her eyes. This is how I would draw her. "Stay with me for a bit?" she asks.

We linger like this until the sky is a bright baby blue and the morning's first pack of surfers have paddled out. Inside the house everyone is still sleeping. As Petra heads to her room, I want to call out and invite her into our bed just so she doesn't have to be alone.

I watch her go and listen as she gently shuts her bedroom door. I hear the taps turn for a bath. In my room, I slip out of my sandy clothes and curl into Oliver's warm body, which feels more and more like home.

Chapter Fourteen

"I never thought anyone would actually draw me." Kirby smiles as we settle onto a bench, tucked away in Petra's garden.

By eight A.M., Oliver had been awake and invited me for a run on the beach.

"I'm not a *completely* new person," I teased and kissed him goodbye.

I wandered through the house, the kitchen already bustling with caterers and a team of florists at work on the deck. I found my sketchbook, then Kirby, and asked if she was still up for being my model.

"I've never been drawn before." She adjusts her T-shirt, tucking it into her shorts, then crosses her legs at the ankle. "Can I give it to Liam?"

"Only if you want to steal my wedding gift idea."

Kirby laughs nervously and pulls at the hem of her shorts.

"You okay?"

"Nervous, maybe? You inspire me. I know what that sounds like, but it's true. My mom taught me about how to behave in any situation and which colors work for my skin tone but never sex. No, cancel that. We did talk about sex, just never talked about pleasure." She watches me as I draw, starting with the perfect slope of her nose. "I just don't want to start off on the wrong foot."

"Smart," I say, though I'm not entirely sure what she means.

"Last night, I told Liam about one of my fantasies. It was a dream, really. I'm on a game show and the ultimate prize is sex onstage, in front of the audience. And Liam comes out from backstage and I spin the wheel. It sounds . . . well, it's supposed to be for fun and the fantasy involves him, so I thought he'd be flattered. But he got weird and quiet and pretended he fell asleep. What's that about? We've listened to every fantasy on the site and he's loved them all."

I study her face. The way she bites at her lip trying to mask her disappointment. The way her expression changes so quickly to cover her emotion. "Maybe we should record yours?"

She smiles. "My fantasy?" She crinkles her nose. "But then I'd have to edit my own voice. I hate the sound of my voice."

"Have you ever met someone who does? Like the sound of their own voice?"

She laughs. "Someone must. You're right. Maybe I gift Liam the drawing and the recording."

By noon, Petra's hair and makeup team is set up. After they've made me up to look the most awake I've looked in a long time, and as they start on Kirby and Alicia, I slip away in search of Liam.

I find him upstairs, hiding in the infrared sauna, fully clothed. "Don't worry, it's not on," he says.

"What's going on? I thought you would be first in line for the cotton candy machine." I sit beside him on the sauna's cedar bench.

"There's a cotton candy machine?" he asks, lifting his head of curls. "Never mind. That's not important."

"Are you upset?"

"Nope. Because if I was, you might use it to make a point about getting married too soon."

"Ha ha."

When he doesn't say more, I gently nudge his leg with mine.

"Obviously," he relents. "I am ready to be married. But. Yes. Maybe I did have a moment of wondering why she's with me. And yes, feeling freaked out about our sex life, okay? I'm a cliché. Or a hypocrite. Both?" In a softer voice he adds, "I just worry she wants more."

"More of what?"

"Just everything—more . . . somebody else."

"Right." We sit in silence for a minute. "Liam. We're all scared most of the time. And if you're not, you're a weird robot. With probably much bigger problems." I study his profile, the gentle angles of his face. "You're enough for everyone you meet. Sometimes, you're even too much."

Liam groans but with a wide grin.

I gently nudge his leg again. "Are you sure this thing isn't on? I feel like I'm sweating from the inside out."

"It might be," he confesses.

I take his hand and hold it on my lap.

"Your palm is really sweaty," he complains. "What? It is."

"Have you felt yours? Shut up. Three things, okay?"

He rolls his eyes, but his smile is tender and sweet. "I'm listening."

"One, I love you."

He sighs. "I love you too. But sometimes you're incredibly annoying."

"I know. Number two. I'm really happy for you and Kirby and I'd love to be a part of your wedding. If it's okay with Kirby? I want to help celebrate you both."

"Of course."

"But don't make me do a weird reading about the wind always being at your back during the ceremony."

"Do you even know me?"

"Three. Kirby is very cool. And also very, very lucky. And also my makeup is melting off and we have to get out of here so you can fix it."

The guests pour in downstairs. They are here for me and to celebrate Dirty Diana, but also not. They're here for one of Petra's famous beach parties. They're here to be photographed. They're here to play on the beach.

"Nervous?" Oliver asks, wrapping a calming arm around me.

"Excited."

"Me too. Look what you created. From the seed of an idea. And now everyone will understand how incredible you are. Besides my parents, of course."

"Of course." I laugh.

Oliver slips away to get us drinks and I stay behind to peek at the entryway, now with a line of people waiting to make their way in. All these many months I've spent hiding Dirty Diana, worried about who will find out I'm involved when or who will react in what way—and now, with the arrival of each guest, another layer of my trepidation falls away, making room for celebration.

At the front of the line, a woman with long strawberry-colored hair, a little older than me, shifts her weight from one foot to the other.

She looks lost so I welcome her in and ask if I can get her a drink.

"Oh, I'm not staying. Thank you."

"Are you sure? It might be fun."

"I shouldn't even be here. I have loads of work. My computer beckons."

"I hear you. But you drove all the way out here from . . ."

"Studio City. I guess I wouldn't mind some fresh air." She hesitates, not seeming to see anyone she knows, so I walk her outside to sit on the beach. She plants herself in the sand and closes her eyes, takes a gulp of the ocean air.

"Can I tell you something?" she asks. "I ate some mushroom chocolate someone gave me. It was supposed to be a microdose. To help my social anxiety. It kicked in ten minutes ago and I don't know if this is normal, but it feels like I'm swimming through lava and your nose seems like it's gently slipping off your face."

"Oh," I say. That explains her unsteady behavior.

"The air feels excellent, though."

"Then let's stay out here for a minute."

"Isn't this your party? You shouldn't be babysitting me. Unless you want some of this chocolate?"

"No, thank you. I could use the fresh air, too."

"I'm a people watcher, really. I prefer to sit in a nice little corner and watch. But I don't think I could get to that corner at the moment. I'd love to ride in on that dolphin. Wouldn't that be amazing?"

"I could help you find a nice corner?"

She gets to her feet, a little wobbly. "If I wasn't so stoned, I'd be embarrassed."

"We've all been there," I say, wrapping my arm around her waist for support.

As we make our way through the party and upstairs, she asks, "Do you think I need a French braid? I have this vision in my head that I'm wearing a French braid."

"I can do a French braid."

She smiles. "I like your company."

"Thank you."

"You're just like you advertise. You make people feel normal even when they want to ride into your party on a dolphin."

Guests continue to arrive and as I make my way through the heart of the party in search of Oliver, someone calls, "Diana!" I turn and try to place her, a freckled, brunette stranger. "I love your site," she tells me. "We listen to the fantasies religiously."

"Thank you." I smile. My first time being recognized. I can feel my cheeks go pink. "That's so nice to hear."

"Your voice! I can't believe it's you!" her friend joins in. They ask me to sign something—anything—then offer up a pen and a Dirty Diana cocktail napkin, laughing. I happily sign it for them, and as I make my way to the deck, the buzzy thrill of the party thrums through me.

I find L'Wren and Arthur outside.

"What is happening here?" L'Wren asks, sweeping me into a hug. "You've turned into Barbie living in Barbie Dreamhouse. Where's Ken?"

"I was hoping you would know. Arthur, I'm so glad you came!"

I walk them down toward the beach. L'Wren takes an ahi tuna on crispy rice from every caterer we pass. "I haven't eaten since the Dallas airport." Once she has sampled her fill, she pulls me aside. "Okay. I'll start with the most important item. The blue one. That's the one. My god, is that *the one*."

"You tried the vibrator?"

"We wore it out. I mean. It may not be able to hold a charge anymore. Arthur wasn't even threatened. It made the whole thing even more fun. We're in a throuple with a vibrator!"

"I'm so happy for all three of you."

"Where's Liam? Is he dressed appropriately? I sent him with a linen suit from Saks and labeled which shirt."

"I think I saw him upstairs."

I turn back to the growing party and nearly knock into Petra, who is beaming with hostess energy. "Have you done the step and repeat?"

"Like the dance?"

"Oh, Diana." L'Wren heads off to find Liam, and Petra leads me through the house to the garden, where a healthy crowd has lined up to have their photographs taken against the Dirty Diana backdrop. Petra cuts the line and places us both in front of flashing cameras. "Smile!" I watch her out of the corner of my eye and try to mimic her effortlessness. It's easy to draft off Petra's energy. Like always, I feel more alive when I'm near her and especially tonight, celebrating something we built.

After a few pictures, we happily make our way back through the party. She says hello to everyone as we go, never getting stuck in any one conversation for too long.

Over the music Petra tells me, "Vibezz is here. Or at least the CEO is. Margot. Her assistant texted to let me know that she ate a mushroom chocolate." Petra laughs. "You're going to love her."

"Oh." The people watcher. "I know where she is." I lead Petra to a small nook that overlooks the living room. Margot is there, surrounded by party snacks and chatting with Liam.

"Margot??" Petra yells a little too loudly. "Can you sit up?"

Margot beams when she sees me. "Thank you for checking up on me."

"I'm so glad you two met."

"Yes, Diana, this is a great party."

"Would you like to stay here? In this nook?" Petra asks, again too loudly.

"She's on 'shrooms, not hard of hearing," Liam says.

"I'm having the best time being here, watching. Liam is telling me about his parents' divorce. It's lovely." Margot looks blissful.

"Can we answer any questions for you?" Petra asks. "About the site?"

"Nope. Diana told me everything I needed to know when she found me this spot."

"Oh. Wonderful. Anything else we can get you?" Petra asks.

"I overheard someone mention cotton candy?"

"I'm on it," Liam says.

I lean in to shake Margot's hand. "I look forward to working together," I say.

Petra and I giggle all the way down the stairs. "Do you think she'll remember how much she likes you? Maybe we should have her sign the contract now?"

Downstairs, Petra takes in the party and sighs. "Now, back to my swan song."

"Swan song?" I stop midstep and just as I do, a woman in a bright pink dress clutches my arm. "I love your site! I'm next, I swear. I have to be." She squeezes my shoulder and keeps walking, straight for the middle of the dance floor. Her compliment makes me dizzy. Or maybe it's being recognized again. Or the music getting louder. Or Petra's news.

"Are you leaving?" I ask her.

"Diana, this is all you." She smiles. "I will always be here when you need help, but you can take the wheel now."

"I can't take the wheel. I don't know how to do any of this!"

"Of course you do. None of this would have happened without you. I was just a good hire."

A woman I swear is one of the Housewives bumps into me, spilling her drink down my arm, but I barely feel it.

The music gets louder and Petra shouts to be heard over it. "I got you on the map. But you know how to stay here."

"I don't. I can barely find Oliver at this party."

"The truth is it's time for me to think seriously about Mitch's legacy. He had so much he wanted to do. All these communities he wanted to serve with the money he made. I'm finally ready to help."

"Are we breaking up in the middle of our party?"

"No. We're celebrating how far we've come."

"Petra—"

"Don't look behind you. Just smile."

I immediately turn to look.

Jasper is standing beside two women taller than he is. One has a thick, shiny ponytail. They both look twenty. He spots me just as Petra is pulled away by another guest.

"Hi!" I say. "You came." I'm trying to cover my shock.

"I hope that's okay?"

"Yes. Of course. But. I wasn't sure." Again I scan the room for Oliver.

"This is Libby and Maria." But Maria has already grown bored and drifted toward the dance floor.

"Hi, Libby."

She has a very strong handshake.

"Their teammates have rented a place just down the beach for the summer."

"Teammates?"

"Beach volleyball," Libby says. She casually admires the house. "Beautiful place."

"It's not mine. But thank you. Maybe you can start a volleyball game at back?"

"Maybe." She looks at me as if I just suggested she clean up all the used cups. "Is that Natalie Hutton?"

"Oh yes, she's a friend of . . . well, sort of mine."

Jasper grins. "I knew Diana before she threw parties for movie stars. When she was living in a sweet little studio apartment with a broken sink and no real dishes."

Is he flirting with me? All we did in that studio apartment was have sex. Libby has spotted someone and is dragging Jasper away.

"I'll catch up with you later," Jasper promises.

Feeling shunned, I go in search of Oliver and bump into Natalie Hutton.

"I heard you had a great meeting with Allison!" she exclaims, scooping me into her arms.

"Oh, good! It was a little hard to tell."

"I love a mystery."

"Me too."

"Me too," she repeats.

"Sorry?"

"Sorry?" she apes. "I'm trying to get your intonation right. You have such interesting mannerisms. And the slightest lisp."

"I have a lisp?"

"Barely noticeable. But it's what I do. *Listhp.* Do you realize that's how you said it?"

"I did?"

"I'd love to meet Oliver if he's here."

"He is somewhere . . ." Where is he?

"And you bite your cuticles! Wonderful. All the little details will really bring this character to life when I play you. Is that Libby Hoffman?"

"Who?"

"The volleyball player." I follow her gaze to Libby, standing near Jasper at the edge of the dance floor.

"Oh right. I think so."

"Well, if you feel eyes burning into you, it's just me doing a little actor homework."

"Okay," is all I can think to say as she heads over to Libby.

Suddenly the crowd in front of me parts, and Alicia, fresh from the ocean, grabs me by the waist.

"This party is too bananas. The setting. The people watching. Oliver and Jasper. My worlds are colliding."

"Your worlds?"

"I meant yours. Do you think Jasper brought the Olympians to make you jealous?"

"They were in the Olympics?"

"Silver medal."

"No. I think he brought her because she's gorgeous. And talented. And very strong."

"And to make you a tiny bit jealous. Did it work?"

"Maybe. Natalie Hutton says I have a lisp."

Alicia considers me.

"I don't, right?" I ask.

"Repeat after me: She sells seashells—"

"Shut up."

"So the movie is happening?"

"Who knows. But I think Petra might be leaving me."

"Leaving you or Dirty D?"

"Dirty Diana."

"Smart. It's time."

"It's not time! We just started!"

"Look around, Diana. Things are deeply in motion."

"Can I ask you something?"

"With that adorable lisp? Anything."

"Would you ever direct the fantasies? If we shot them for the site."

"Me?"

"I realize every time Liam brings it up, I picture this mustached lothario directing them and I think that is why I keep saying no. But if you directed them, I would be excited."

"You had me at 'would you.'"

"Yeah?"

"Look at us at a Malibu party making our own Hollywood deals."

...

I finally spot Oliver across the dance floor, and when we meet eyes, he excuses himself and heads right to me. "Can I talk to you for a sec?"

"Is everything okay?" I ask.

His eyebrows knit together. "Yeah. I just have something for you."

"Where have you been? I've been looking for you."

"Yeah?" He seems excited.

"Where were you?"

"You'll see."

When we reach the bedroom, Oliver closes the door behind us, the party noise immediately muffled.

"Come here," he says. His jaw is tight, but his eyes are lit with mischief.

I move toward him until we're inches apart. His arms stay at his sides, but I can hear his breath go ragged. He lifts my chin but instead of kissing me, he traces his fingers down my neck to my shoulder. He slips the straps of my dress from my shoulders and I let it fall to the floor. He reaches into the back pocket of his shorts and pulls out the handcuffs. He slips a cuff around my left wrist and snaps it shut.

"Oliver?" Standing in my bra and underwear, I can hear partygoers on the other side of the door. A thrill runs through me. The thumping music, the laughing and high-pitched voices.

I expect him to cuff the other hand. I'm picturing him exploring my body while I'm unable to touch him, his face between my thighs, his tongue inside me. Already I want to grab him and pull him onto me, into me.

But he doesn't cuff my hands together or pull us onto the bed.

Without taking his eyes from mine, he leads me into the bathroom, the cuffs dangling from my left wrist. He looks at the cool marble floor. "Sit here."

I'm too excited to question him, as if following directions gets me one step closer to his hands on me. I kneel on the hard ground, my face level with his hips. I reach my uncuffed hand for the button of his shorts—but he stops me. He gets on his knees before me, leans in, and kisses my mouth. His lips are soft and salty, his kiss hard and urgent. I explode with want, leaning deep into his kiss. But he pulls away, fast. "Not yet," he whispers and snaps the empty cuff around a pipe, handcuffing me to the sink.

"What are you doing?"

Oliver stands. "I'll be back."

Oliver leaves me alone. Handcuffed to the sink. I can hear the party outside. Make out the noises. The laughter. I hear Natalie Hutton. And L'Wren.

For the first several minutes, I stay seated on the floor, leaning against the wall and steadying my breath. I start to worry about missing Petra's party—she threw this for Dirty Diana after all, shouldn't Diana be out there? Then I realize, my work here is done. Margot is being taken care of and everyone is having a good time.

I decide to take a dose of my own medicine: to be handcuffed to a sink by Oliver, to feel so desired by him and to want him so hungrily in return—this is what I've been wanting. I relax into the sensation, turning off my mind and dropping into my body. Time slows as I wait for Oliver to come back. I shift on the hard floor, and the more uncomfortable I become, the more aroused, my blood pumping even harder at the thought of Oliver appearing in the doorframe. But several long minutes pass and there is no sign of him. There is a circular mirror above the sink, framed by a larger, square window. The cuff can glide along the pipe so it's easy for me to stand and look outside. I look in the mirror first—I study my face, my lips swollen from his rough kiss—and then out the window. I can't see the patio or any of the guests from here, but I have a clear view of the beach. I see partygoers in the ocean, most of them up to their knees along the shore. And then I make out Oliver, his navy-blue shorts. To my surprise, he's playing football.

With Jasper.

Like two handsome cousins reunited on their Kennebunkport lawn, not a regular-person care in the world.

Oliver runs into the shallow surf to catch a spiral. He must know I'm watching. Of course he does. He peels off his shirt and tosses it onto the sand, then throws the ball long. And instead of letting it crash into the ocean, Jasper runs in after it. He catches it then emerges, laughing and soaked, and strips off his own shirt.

Someone I don't recognize comes to join them, then a fourth, and eventually Oliver and Jasper step away from the game, wandering up toward the party, Jasper's arm is draped casually over Oliver's shoulder. Near the house, I lose sight of them.

The tingling in my body returns. Oliver is coming for me.

I slide down to the floor and wait, picturing him finding me—still wet from the ocean, salty and warm from the sun.

Minutes pass and still he doesn't come. The bathroom is cold and tiled and I shift my weight trying to get comfortable. I close my eyes and imagine Oliver coming for me. I can't wait for him. I slip my fingers beneath my underwear. I move them slowly, the warm sensation building in my groin, when I hear the bedroom door open. Oliver. I sit up.

"Finally," I call as the bathroom door opens. But the figure in the doorway is not Oliver.

Jasper furrows his brows and takes in the scene—me, almost naked, handcuffed to the sink. He opens his mouth but nothing comes out. As much as I want to disappear, once he locks his eyes on mine, I can't look away. He bites down on his bottom lip, a flash of desire in his eyes. I can feel the same in mine. But it's all wrong. We've been miscast and these aren't our roles anymore.

My mouth is dry, my cheeks burning. "I'll see you at the party?" I say, as if he'd just caught me touching up my lipstick.

He smiles and nods. "See you there." When the bedroom door closes, I manage to connect my foot with the bathroom door and I slam it shut.

A few minutes later, Oliver appears. He's damp with sweat, or ocean water.

"Undo the handcuffs. Now."

Oliver pauses, an expression in his eyes like he wants to devour me whole. "You really want me to?"

My own need to feel his hands on me flashes through me, and I shake my head no. Oliver bends down and reaches for the strap of my bra, a smile playing at the corners of his mouth. I'm coursing with desire. So powerful I want to bottle it and save it for a rainy day back in Dallas after the dust has settled. When I'm not half naked and shivering with need in a beachfront mansion bathroom.

The sex is fast and explosive. Oliver was hard the minute he entered the room and once our bodies finally meet, after lying in wait for what felt like hours, the pleasure is overwhelming.

"I need this," I tell him. I spread my legs so he can push deeper inside me, again and again. I try to hold off but it feels too good.

"I need this too," Oliver says and comes with me.

The rest of the party we float. Separating and mingling and then finding each other, brushing up against each other.

At one point, I spot Oliver deep in conversation with Jasper, the two of them near the outdoor fireplace. I linger within earshot to find them having a strangely intense conversation about sneakers.

As the party wears on, I slip away to FaceTime Emmy. She complains, briefly, about the red, white, and blue ensemble Vivian made her wear, but then carries the phone into the kitchen to show off the red, white, and blue cupcakes they made. I can hear Vivian and Allen's own party in the background and Emmy tells me she needs to go, Grandpa and sparklers are waiting on her.

I check in on Margot just as she emerges from her nook like a hibernating bear, happily taking in the party she missed.

"Margot!" I call. I give her a thumbs-up. "Everything good?"

"I had the best time! And Liam is a gem. Should we set a call and get into details next week?"

"I'd like that."

"We're going to do great things in this space, Diana. I'll let Petra know."

Another thumbs-up, this one with tears in my eyes.

I head to the balcony to take in the spectacular party. The beach is still full of happy guests, a surreal mix of well-dressed people on the other side of the glass doors, sipping cocktails, wiping their mouths with napkins printed with a Dirty Diana logo. I want to remember this exact moment, alone in a crowd, dreamlike and fleeting. Quickly checking to make sure no one is watching, I take out my phone and snap a selfie.

"I can get a better shot, if you want."

"I got it. Thanks." My cheeks burn a deep red with embarrassment.

"No judgment. I have the exact same shot outside every gallery I've been a part of. It's impressive. All this."

Jasper's clothes have dried; his thick, dark hair is perfectly in place. He rocks back on his heels, his mouth turning up in a small smile. "I was ready to call 911 earlier. Just so you know."

I laugh, the blush reaching to the tips of my ears. "Thanks. For looking after me."

"Diana . . ." He stops, a look of pure tenderness in his eyes. "I like Oliver."

"Me too."

"I can tell." Then, standing up straighter, he says, "You two should stop by my place tomorrow. It's just down the road. I might take out my neighbor's boat and sail to Catalina. Have you been?"

"No."

"Might be a fun day." Then he adds, "A double date."

"Yeah, maybe."

"Come on. Where's your sense of adventure?" Jasper teases. "Oliver would say yes."

"Would he?"

"Watch this," he says confidently.

We peer over the deck to where Oliver is laughing with Alicia in the sand. "Hey, Oliver! Want to sail to Catalina tomorrow? On my neighbor's boat?"

Oliver takes a sip of his beer and grins. "Sure, buddy."

Jasper turns back to me and beams. "See? We're buddies."

My fantasy is change. I want everything to be different. I want my girlfriend to touch me differently, I want to feel differently when she does touch me. I want to know that we can still evolve into better lovers. I want her to get bit by a radioactive spider and turn into an intuitive sex superhero. Maybe then she would try something different when her face is between my legs. Maybe one day she dresses up as Harley Quinn and pins me naked to the bed.

PART THREE

Catalina, California

Chapter Fifteen

The next morning Oliver is out of bed by 5:30, claiming he's still on Texas time. I suspect he has been awake for a while, mulling Jasper's offer. I could feel him thinking as he lay next to me. Now he calls casually from the tiny bathroom, "We should go. I've always wanted to see Catalina." As if Catalina were Maui or Monaco.

Petra catches wind of the plan and practically books the hotel and packs our overnight bags for us. "The party did everything we hoped! We celebrated Dirty Diana, we had fun, and Margot and her piles of money want to work with us. Go!"

Jasper tells us his date is already on the island so it will be just the three of us sailing together. For all the ways it feels wrong, and there are many, it also feels strangely right. These two men, here together— one bold and unpredictable, the other kindhearted and sensitive. They have made an effort to get along. For my sake. I'm not sure I understand fully, but I am trying to appreciate the gesture. I've never heard either of them mention an interest in sailing, and yet, yesterday at the party—after they had exhausted the topic of favorite soccer players—they spent an hour sharing fantasies of living on a boat. Oliver had a summer of sailing camp as a teenager. Jasper learned how to sail on an eighteen-day trip from Mexico to French Polynesia. Both harbored a childhood dream of sailing all alone to a distant land. Like Robert Redford in *All Is Lost*.

While Jasper mans the wheel, Oliver stands at the mast, admiring the wide expanse of the Pacific Ocean. The wind blows through our hair, and all around us the water sparkles. If it makes anyone else feel electric, they don't share it with me. We are like three happy friends, without any history, off for a day's adventure. As we get closer to Catalina, somehow this new story of us is falling into place. We have raised the sails and caught a decent wind, and soon the waves start to pick up. Oliver turns to me, suddenly pale. "I'm feeling it."

Jasper strides toward him. "You okay, buddy?"

I'm torn between comforting my husband and taking the wheel. Jasper decides for me.

"Don't let us drift." When I start to protest, he says, "It's just like a car."

Oliver turns to Jasper, slightly embarrassed. "I don't usually get seasick," he says.

"Happens to the best of us," Jasper tells him. "Keep taking deep breaths."

Oliver wraps his hands around the railing and Jasper places a hand on the small of his back.

"You'll be all right," Jasper says. He is being attentive. Like he used to be with me. After a few minutes, Jasper takes the wheel again. I sit beside Oliver and he lays his head in my lap. He closes his eyes and takes in gulps of fresh air. His face is already pink from the sun, accentuating his blue-green eyes. I stroke his hair, streaked with copper from the sun. When I look at Jasper, he is watching us both.

As we approach the island, a young man in a harbormaster boat pulls alongside us. He asks for a reservation number and waves us toward the moorings with a pleasant smile. We exit the boat to a quaint, stony seaside town. Oliver finds a bench to sit on, and Jasper and I go in search of coffee. By the time we return, Oliver has revived and is eating a bag of saltwater taffy.

We make our way down a crowded sidewalk, my arm in Oliver's, and then, after we almost lose each other in the pedestrian traffic, the other arm in Jasper's. I have the pleasant sensation of the boat's constant rocking still with me. I feel the pavement rolling underfoot as we walk. We pass several ice cream parlors and browse the unframable seaside art. Jasper holds up a piece of distressed wood with LOVE GROWS HERE branded onto it. I'm drawn to a small pastel drawing of seagulls against a vivid sunset. I can't tell if I like it. The charm of the whole day is rattling me.

The air smells of fried food and seawater. We stop for fish tacos and cold beers at a restaurant with a large open patio. It's been awhile since Oliver made a new friend, I realize, watching him and Jasper get to know each other. They keep discovering new subjects, new things in common. And just when I begin to feel like a third wheel on someone else's date, I'll notice one of them looking at me, with a quick flash of desire.

"When will we meet Kendra?" I ask Jasper.

"Tonight. If you're up for a party?"

"Kendra is your girlfriend?" Oliver asks.

"Yes." Jasper flags down a waiter and orders a bottle of white wine. "Sort of. She's also my agent. It's a long story."

Our waiter pours a glass for Jasper to taste. "Mmm. This is nice. Try this."

Jasper hands Oliver his glass of wine and he takes a sip, his lips hitting the exact same spot on the glass. I remember a time when Oliver didn't even like sharing a drinking glass with Emmy, wary of her preschool germs.

"Really good," Oliver says. He passes the glass to me and I take a small sip. It is surprisingly good—cold and citrusy. Maybe it's the setting. Maybe we've all relaxed into a California-inspired bliss.

We drink wine and laugh like old friends. Oliver is telling stories about playing football in high school. Jasper leans in.

"You were the homecoming king *and* you went to prom with the prom queen?"

"We were heavily adorned." Oliver chuckles.

"And what is she doing now? The Prom Queen?"

"She contacted me a few years ago, actually. Wanted to meet for a drink. Fresh off a divorce."

I sit up and look at Oliver. "You didn't tell me that? She called you?"

"I know. I'm sorry." Oliver looks sheepish.

"Did you meet her?"

"I'm so sorry. I actually did." His tone is so gleeful, like a kid caught doing something nice, that we all laugh like this is the funniest thing we've ever heard. "We had a drink at the Mansion at Turtle Creek. I was just curious."

"About what?" I ask.

"I guess . . . If she would look at me like she used to."

"Did she?"

Oliver nods.

I can't help it. I feel a flash of jealousy. "And nothing happened?"

"No, of course not." He squeezes my hand. Then sighs. "I just wanted to remember what it felt like."

Oliver changes the subject back to Jasper's life. He wants to know if Jasper worries he could ruin a relationship with his agent by getting romantic, but Jasper laughs. "Oliver. I'm not trying to make it in Hollywood. I really only signed with her hoping to date her. I've never had a single meeting out of it—but she does know all the best parties.

Right now she's chasing Ricky Mazar." Then, he adds, for my sake, "The soccer star. She's asking for my help signing him, you know, likes me there to make her look good. She's fun. You'll love her."

Our hotel is a squat building set against the scrubby hills, which have a sort of angelic softness in the afternoon light. The sky is tinged pink. We head to our rooms to shower and change. Kendra has invited us all to a party in a house on the hill, which she promises will be full of soccer players, including Ricky Mazar, of course, and maybe some of his teammates. Oliver is giddy with excitement, and a little bit tipsy from lunch, as we unpack our clothes on the bed.

"I like Jasper," Oliver says.

"I can see that."

"Yeah?"

"It's nice."

"It's not weird?"

"No."

"I wouldn't blame you. If you still had feelings for him." There's no accusation in his voice, no jealousy. Just intrigue.

"I like being around him," I admit. "But the need for him is not the same."

Oliver smiles.

I spend more time in the shower than usual. Carefully shaving and buffing my skin until it's silky soft to the touch. I blow out my hair and take the time to put on a smoky eye.

We can walk to the party, in a large many-tiered house carved into the side of the island. When we get inside, the lights are low, and it looks as though the party has been going on for days. Every available surface is covered with scattered clothing and abandoned cocktails. The beds are all unmade, satin sheets sliding off the bed frames, and there are wet towels draped over the barstools, the arms of the sofas, and the lawn chairs outside. Long striped bench cushions have been tossed around the wide lawn.

Several waiters in bow ties make their way smoothly around the pool area, silver trays and champagne flutes suggesting a certain formality, but the dress code is all over the place. People are in business suits and cocktail dresses or bikinis and shorts and flip-flops. By now everyone has made the party their own.

A woman rushes up to us to ask Jasper for a favor. Her light brown hair is tied up with a velvet ribbon. Her deep green blouse brings out her eyes. Jasper laughs. "Here's Kendra," he says, just as she reaches out to shake Oliver's hand. Oliver smiles, and his face tightens. It's just barely visible, but I can see he takes an instant dislike to her.

"Lovely to meet you," she says and then turns to me. "Sorry about the chaos." She giggles. "It's kind of a rowdy crowd."

A tall man with a handsome, hawklike face appears next to her and she titters again. "Just who I mean." She introduces us to the soccer player we've heard so much about. "This is Ricky," she says, sounding very proud of him.

Moments after being introduced, Oliver launches into an elaborate set of compliments. He seems to remember Ricky's recent matches with alarming specificity. Even Jasper can perfectly recall several plays. Kendra squeals with laughter as they indulge in an enthusiastic reenactment of one of the match's worst moments, and then she expertly changes the subject. "There's a new plan for tomorrow," she tells Jasper. "Ricky met a captain who drives a yacht that once belonged to Spencer Tracy. He's offered to take us around the island."

"A yacht?" Jasper says.

"Nothing too fancy but old and beautiful," Kendra says.

"We leave in the afternoon," Ricky says, emptying the rest of a bottle of champagne into his glass. "Lunch at the island's best hamburger place, and then a trip on a sailboat."

Kendra gazes at Jasper with real intensity. She rests a hand lightly on his chest. "I hope you'll come with us." Then she turns to Ricky and takes his arm. "I need to introduce you to a few more people, then we're done, I promise." Ricky follows her dutifully. Jasper and Oliver and I find a spot to sit by the pool. Jasper settles into a pool chair next to mine and then he pops back up and goes in search of Kendra. Through the glass doors of the house I watch him trail her for a lap around the large living room, while she introduces Ricky to one cluster of guests after another.

I stretch out on my lounge chair and eavesdrop on a small group of women. I'm trying to puzzle out their connection to one another, as they trade off spilling over with emotion in hushed tones. They don't seem to know one another, I realize. They're all just wasted.

Oliver clutches my arm. He looks like he's seen a ghost and squeezes my fingers. A server in a short black jacket hands him a fresh glass of champagne. Oliver breathes hotly in my ear. "It's Harrison For—or never mind. Nope. I thought it was."

The wine we drank that afternoon has had no effect on me, as if somehow being around both Oliver and Jasper at the same time has kept me vigilant. Deciding to get drunk, I make myself a large vodka tonic, and then I head up to the house to take a look around. There's a stunning painting above one of the fireplaces, a small, brightly colored abstract, but throughout the rest of the downstairs I find only a collection of large framed movie posters, nothing special. I make my way back to the vivid canvas I first saw in the living room. I feel like I should recognize the artist but don't.

"It's a Helen Fread," Jasper says, suddenly at my side. "She was in her eighties when she painted it." We take it in together for a few moments, and then he wraps an arm around my waist and leads me into the next room. Loud, cheerful music is playing from huge speakers in the corner, and several couples are dancing. The woman with the blue scarf now has it doubled around her neck as she weaves drunkenly and unapologetically into Jasper. He smiles and moves me gently out of her path, pulling me to him with a happy confidence. "I love parties," he says. It feels good to be close to him again. Like remembering the best parts of a vacation. We feel comfortable in each other's arms. And I'm keenly aware of the envious eyes of other women. He will never not be admired.

"I like your husband," Jasper says.

"He said the same about you."

"It's weird we get along so well."

I smile but say nothing, swaying with him to the music.

"What is going on in that brain of yours?" Jasper asks. "Are you concocting a dangerous plan?"

"Maybe you're the one with the plan."

"Maybe Oliver's the one with the plan."

Oliver is dancing now, too, with the other party guests. Laughing, his head tilted to the starry sky like he is having genuine fun.

Jasper looks over my shoulder for Kendra. He has a small bruise on the left side of his chin.

I turn, too, and spot her being charming in a crowd. *Oh, Jasper,* I think. I can see he's starting to suffer from Kendra's neglect.

"Great fucking song," Jasper says. I lean into him, letting myself imagine another time, another place, where I could raise my chin and meet his lips, kissing him softly. Jasper senses this and immediately looks for Oliver. "Where's our friend?" he says, gesturing for Oliver to join us.

"You two lovebirds dance," Jasper says, clapping Oliver on the shoulder. "I'll be right back."

Oliver is generally a mushy drunk. Touchy and sentimental. But this time his shoulders are back, not caved in. He pulls me into him. His eyes dazzle. He feels so alive. As if the moment we kiss, we will combust and shatter.

"I liked watching you two dance," Oliver says.

"Did you?" I rest the side of my face against his chest, breathing deeply.

After a sweetly sloppy slow dance, Oliver and I head outside to refresh our drinks and relax by the pool. Oliver strikes up a conversation with a woman in a blue-flowered dress. I settle into my chair cushion and briefly close my eyes. An image of Jasper from the past, from the first night I felt I really knew him—working in the darkroom of that little house in Santa Fe—flashes through my thoughts. I know this is happening because I was just dancing with him, because I'm now feeling close to him again, or remembering that feeling. It's fleeting but nice.

"I like L.A.," I hear Oliver telling the woman next to him. "There's no preconceived idea of anyone. The billboards have pictures of people who have transformed, not balding accident attorneys like in Texas."

Oliver turns and looks at me. "I have an idea. We should move out here," he says. The sober tone makes me laugh.

"I'm so serious," he says.

"This is the third time you've told me that tonight. Let's see how we feel in the morning."

"I've told you already?" Oliver turns back to the woman on his other side. "I haven't convinced her yet," he says.

"Will you go visit the bison while you're here?" she asks us. "They roam wild. Started with fourteen bison brought here from a Texas ranch in the 1920s to be extras in a Hollywood movie, and they've been here ever since. Stuck on the island."

The party rumbles on. At around one in the morning, one of the servers comes back around with tiny sandwiches. "Are these tea sandwiches?" a tall woman in a terry cloth dress and flip-flops asks him. "Focaccia squares," says the waiter. "Oh, I wish it was pizza," someone says. Someone else jumps into the pool fully clothed, and nearby, a server is disrobing and about to join. It's late enough now that only the seriously drunk remain, most of them making out with each other.

I pass a dark corner and see that the woman in the flip-flops has pressed herself against someone and is nuzzling his neck. In another dark corner, I'm only slightly surprised to see Kendra with her arms wrapped around Ricky's neck, kissing him passionately.

In a flash, I turn toward the spot I last saw Jasper, which takes me back through most of the house. There is no sign of him. It's only when I'm almost at the front door that I spot him in the hallway.

"I think an Irish exit might be called for," he says when I reach him. He has wrapped a long green scarf around his neck, and his face is pale.

We gather Oliver and head for the door. Once outside, we run down the long driveway as though someone were chasing us. We head through residential streets back toward the center of town. The night is warm. The moon is full and bright. I take off my heels so I don't fall behind. We are all still letting loose in life, I find myself thinking. Later in life than I would have guessed when I was young. When I finally stop to catch my breath, I realize we are on the sand. Alone. A small inlet, hidden from the rest of the island.

Oliver grins, still high on the party, and pulls me in for a kiss. I taste the champagne on his lips.

Jasper is sitting on a rock, watching us, the moonlight exposing his sharp jawline. "I should have my camera," he says.

"Anyone?" Oliver offers us a sip out of a bottle of champagne.

"Did you swipe this?" I ask, surprised.

"Hey! Jasper stole a scarf!"

"I'll give it back," he says, leaning back and smiling up at the sky. "I swear."

I take a long sip of champagne and feel the bubbles in my throat. Then I pass the bottle to Oliver, who passes it to Jasper. I walk to the water's edge. "I want to swim," I say.

"Careful," Jasper says, but he's grinning. "Watch out for sharks."

"Really?"

"Great whites."

I can't tell if he's serious, but the champagne tells me it's fine either way. "I won't go far."

I lift my dress over my head and toss it onto the sand. I feel young and strong. Like I could swim back to Malibu if I wanted. And when I see how Jasper and Oliver are looking at me, I want to take more off. I play with the thin strap of my bra, teasing. Oliver exhales softly. I unclasp my bra and let it fall to the sand. My breasts are exposed, the crisp air makes my nipples hard. I suddenly miss Texas. The midsummer nights where the air feels like a warm hug. I bend over and slide my underwear off so I'm completely naked in the moonlight. "Coming?" I ask them.

Without hesitating, Oliver unbuttons his shirt and rips off his jeans, following me into the ocean like he doesn't want to miss out on the fun. The shock of the cold water is like an ice bath. I dive underwater and surface to find Oliver beside me. His strong arms pull me into him. I can feel his excitement.

"How can you possibly be this sexy?" he says.

I wrap my legs around his waist, pressing my chest against his. "Keep me warm." *No one will know,* I think to myself, *if I lower my pelvis to meet his. No one will know.*

"How's the water?" Jasper calls.

"Come in and find out," I call back.

Jasper shakes his head, bathed in moonlight, and starts to strip. His shoulders are broad and perfectly toned. As he strides toward us, his powerful arms swinging, Oliver turns to me and whispers. "What's happening?"

"Does it matter?"

"No."

Jasper dives under the water and heads for us, stopping just a few feet away. His hair and eyelashes are black and wet. No one speaks but I can hear us all breathing. I feel dizzy with desire. A feeling of fullness between my legs. I take Jasper's hand and pull him toward me and

Oliver, the warmth of his body heating us like the sun. Then I kiss Oliver. His hands still grip my hips. Our kiss is immediately intense, the urgent kiss of two people shedding their former selves.

Then I turn to Jasper, tentative... One of them will stop me if I've gone too far. But he receives my kiss with such passion that I see colors. Bright explosions of red and orange appear before my closed eyes.

Then I kiss Oliver. Then Jasper again. There is so little space between our lips that the kisses merge, becoming one elongated kiss, and I can only tell the difference between them by the feel of their stubble and the faint smell of whiskey on Jasper's lips. We are spinning and dizzy, walking a once straight line that now curves. Our lips wet with seawater.

I pull Jasper and Oliver toward each other. Their noses touch. Their lips are so close they breathe in the same air. And then Jasper gently tilts Oliver's chin toward his mouth and kisses him. The kiss starts soft and slow but turns into something more urgent, their tongues twisting with desire. I've never been more aroused. After a long minute they break apart, their eyes wild, waiting for their next command.

"Let's go back to the room," I say.

We dress silently on the sand, our clothes clinging to our wet bodies. The walk back to the hotel is quiet. We pass young couples leaving the bars and busboys counting their tips. When we get to our hotel room, Oliver unlocks our door and I step inside. The room is freshly cleaned, and the bed perfectly made.

Jasper hovers at the entrance. My heart pounds in anticipation and I feel giddy with the possibilities of where this night can go, and then Oliver slowly opens the door farther to extend the invitation. Jasper immediately walks to the in-room bar. "What can I get everyone to drink? I have Crown or vodka?"

We clink the tiny glass bottles of alcohol together and down them. The Crown burns my throat. I imagine myself floating over the three of us like a ghost. Oliver and Jasper look at each other, expectant, but still not moving.

I slowly pull my dress up over my hips, exposing my lace underwear, still damp from the ocean. I sit on the edge of the bed and let my legs fall open, daring one of them to touch me. Oliver moves first, his eyes warm with desire. "You're killing me."

He yanks my dress over my head and pulls my lace underwear down, tossing them into our open luggage. He kneels in front of me and my open legs begin to shake. Oliver is in complete control. I'm so taken by his confidence that I almost forget that Jasper is in the room. But then I feel a warm breath on the back of my neck. Jasper is kissing my earlobe tenderly, then sucking on it in the way he knows drives me crazy.

"You're so wet . . ." Oliver says.

I sigh in pleasure as Jasper takes Oliver's position between my legs, parting them even farther. I lie back on the bed, with Jasper between my legs and Oliver watching. When I feel Jasper's warm breath on my inner thigh, I instinctively close my legs. The tiny doubts return. We've gone too far. We won't come back from this. *Dirty.*

But when I look up at Oliver, his eyes are soft. He traces his hand across my chest, pulling my bra down, squeezing my naked breast, then massaging my nipple between his fingers. I feel a rush of excitement, my husband giving my lover permission to please me. All doubts slip away, and my body opens like a flower. Jasper presses his warm tongue inside me and I groan in pleasure. I don't care if I wake the other guests.

"Do you like that?" Oliver asks, never taking his eyes off Jasper's mouth.

"Yes," I say, desperate to feel more of Jasper's tongue inside me. The gentle scratch of his stubble between my legs.

Oliver leans in, his mouth slack, and watches as Jasper uses his entire tongue to lick me from top to bottom. With one hand, I touch Oliver's erection through his jeans, with the other, I run my fingers through Jasper's wet hair, smiling as Jasper devours me.

"Tell him. Tell him you like it," Oliver says, his voice husky.

"I like it," I say. Jasper looks up at Oliver, his lips wet. Oliver reaches his arm across my body, and gently spreads my legs farther apart, so that Jasper can take me all in his mouth. When he does, it is Oliver who moans. My eyes search his face. His cheeks are red, sweat beading on his forehead. "Do you want me to come?" I ask him, breathless.

"So much . . ." he says.

Oliver leans into me and kisses me as Jasper massages me, rhythmically sliding his fingers in and out. He's always known how to touch me. It's been his superpower since we first met. An innate knowledge of how my body worked. My back starts to arch and stiffen as my orgasm slowly takes shape, more powerful than ever before, but I can't let the night end. I need more.

"I want to fuck my husband, now," I tell them, kneeling on the bed. Oliver pulls off his jeans and takes my place, lying down.

"I want your clothes off too," I say to Jasper.

Jasper does as he's told and pulls off his sweater, tossing his pants on top of Oliver's discarded clothes. I smile when I see their pile of clothes, tangled on the hotel floor.

"You're so fucking sexy." Oliver strokes himself, hard again in seconds. Every part of my body needs to be filled so I straddle his hips and guide him inside me. My hands rest on his bare chest. My breath grows ragged. I ride him hard as his hands grip the bedsheets. And when I look up, I see Jasper. We lock eyes as I press my hips into Oliver, playing with different rhythms and speeds. Jasper smiles, his eyes lighting up each time I moan. He leans forward so he can kiss me. I meet his lips, letting Oliver fall out of me, my desire dripping onto his stomach, my legs on either side of him.

Desperate for more of me, Oliver lowers his body so his face is between my legs as Jasper pulls me in for a long kiss.

I feel worshipped. To be their center of attention.

I lower myself back onto Oliver and savor the feeling of him inside me again, riding him slowly and methodically, trying to make the euphoric feeling last all night.

"Diana," Oliver groans.

I raise my pelvis to the most sensitive part of him and slowly lower myself again. Jasper sits directly behind Oliver, stroking himself while watching us. Oliver grimaces in pleasure, turning his head to the side, a plant reaching for the sun, and Jasper's erection grazes his cheek.

It sets us all on fire.

Oliver grips my hips, pressing his fingertips into my ass, so he can pull me into him. I relax my body even more so he can be deeper inside me. If I could fuck both of them at once I would. I'm the center of their world. Both Jasper and Oliver, locked into my pleasure.

"You're so beautiful." Jasper is close.

But it's Oliver who starts to pulse inside me. He's looking in the mirror above the dresser, at the reflection of our three naked bodies. So it won't end, I stop the night in its tracks, letting Oliver slip out of me, so we can start over and find our way back to this place. Rewind the tape to the moment we first gave in to one another, and I replay it over and over again until we combust. Back to the dance floor, to the ocean, to the moment Oliver opens the hotel door another few inches.

I need to be with both of them. No more taking turns. Waiting patiently for the other. The force that draws us together is too powerful. I lie down next to Oliver on the bed. Jasper follows and lies down on my right. Oliver, my left. And within seconds the organization of our tryst flies away and we are tangled inside each other's limbs. I can't tell Oliver's body from Jasper's as the heat of them both seeps into my skin. I'm enclosed in their firm bodies and the world falls away. Everywhere I turn there is muscle and flesh, pleasuring me, sliding in and out of me, kissing me in places that were kept closed and are now open. Their moans merge and echo in my head. My own sounds are unrecognizable, throaty and carnal. Hands and wet lips roam across my body, exploring every inch, every curve of me. Sudden, powerful explosions of pleasure make our bodies slick and bind us together.

We come in waves, falling into a deep swim of ecstasy, then breaking to the surface, and needing even more. Our heat. Our wetness. Our hardness and our softness. They both have me tonight. And I have them.

I wake up the next morning before Oliver does. My entire body is drowsy and satiated, the feeling after a long day in the sun. The details of last night hit me in vivid flashes. I snuggle into Oliver's chest and he brings me in even closer, kissing the top of my head.

"Good morning," I say.

"Good morning," he says.

We are good. We are unbreakable. It feels magnificent.

"Last night . . ." I say, trailing off.

Oliver smiles. "Last night . . ." he repeats.

"Did you have fun?"

"Yes. Did you?"

"Yes."

"Do we need to talk about what it means?" he asks.

"Maybe it means we like having fun."

A light tap at our hotel window interrupts our conversation. It is Jasper. Freshly showered and all smiles.

"Hi, friends," Jasper says.

"Good morning."

"How are we feeling this morning?"

"Good," I say. "You?"

"Very restful night of sleep," Jasper says.

Oliver smiles lazily and wipes the sleep out of his eyes. "Us, too, buddy." He stands up and opens the door so Jasper can poke his head in. "My friend Gina is here. She got in this morning. We're going to take the boat back to Palos Verdes for a few days. You interested?"

I peek out the window and see a slender blonde scrolling on her phone. She looks up and smiles. Oliver looks at me and raises his eyebrows. "That sounds really nice but we have to get back to Texas," he says.

Jasper winks at us and walks over to Gina, wrapping an arm around her waist. "Arrivederci! We'll always have Catalina!" he calls, as they head for the stairs leading down to the sea.

Oliver flops back down on the bed and takes my hand. "When did he meet her?"

"You jealous?" I tease.

"Don't think so," he says, though he seems to mull it. "Where's he get the energy?"

"It's how he copes," I say.

PART FOUR

Home

Chapter Sixteen

On our way to the airport, Oliver and I stop to visit my mother one more time. Her apartment is in a 1950s pink dingbat with an open carport. We bring her Starbucks coffee and blueberry muffins and she gives us a short tour. The decor is so varied that almost anyone could live there. A hand-me-down piano keyboard collects dust in the corner, a French New Wave movie poster is framed above the couch, and an expensive blender squats on her kitchen counter.

There are no pictures of me or Oliver or Emmy. She decided long ago that that role wasn't for her and that is okay. It's the only way she knew how to survive. *It's how she copes.* It's becoming a ritual to say this to myself. She peers into the bag of muffins and sighs. "This is way too many! I'm going to freeze these and have them for breakfast all week!"

I smile at the last-minute jab. We have bought an exorbitant, wasteful number of muffins, she'd like us to know. And we don't seem to care. Must be nice, she wants to say. But she and I hug goodbye without too much tension, and then we're off to the airport.

Oliver's parents and Emmy made it back to Dallas last night and they've already called to warn us the weather is awful, windy with hail in the forecast. We manage to take off on time, but the flight is bumpier than I'd like. Oliver reminds me to breathe through the turbulence. "We're going to be fine. These planes can handle just about anything."

In-flight service is canceled for the remainder of the flight, so I study the flight attendants' faces, looking for a reason to panic. When they look worried, I will allow myself to worry too. But they don't even flinch at the bumps. One hardly looks up from her book.

We land to a weather alert in Dallas, complete with a tornado warning. Huge gusts of wind rock our cab back and forth on the highway home. Billboards advertising pawnshops and the Texas lotto make me miss Los Angeles. The best thing about returning home is Emmy, who is waiting on our doorstep. She runs into my arms, her dress blowing up so far it covers her face. "The flowers burned!" she announces. She's right. The flowers Oliver planted for me before we left couldn't survive the July heat and are now just crispy, charred sticks.

We thank Oliver's parents for doing such a wonderful job and quickly pile them into their car before the weather gets any worse. Just as they head off, the wind picks up a little more. A set of wooden shutters detaches and goes bouncing down our cul-de-sac.

"That won't be cheap," Oliver says.

"Should we wait it out in the basement?" I ask him.

"I don't think it's that serious."

But an alarm on both our phones tells us otherwise. We call Oliver's parents to make sure they've made it home safely then wait out the storm in our murky basement, putting on cheery smiles for

Emmy's sake. After five games of UNO and three confusing rounds of Exploding Kittens, we emerge. The house is eerily quiet. Oliver and I make ourselves busy, unpacking our suitcases, turning on TVs and filling the house with distracting noise.

We put Emmy to bed, and I change into pajamas and brush my teeth. When I come back into our room, Oliver is stretched out on the bed watching Netflix and I am jolted by the familiarity of the scene. What life am I walking back into? We were so close to feeling something different, feeling somehow like we were new . . . and now I feel as though we picked the wrong card in Candyland and are back at the gumdrop.

I squeeze Oliver's shoulder. "Back in your old bed. How does it feel?"

"Maybe we should invest in a new mattress?"

"You want to sleep on the couch?"

"On my first night back? No. That feels weird."

Neither one of us sleeps. Oliver tosses and turns, adjusting various pillows between his legs, and I start to spin out. Is it being back in Texas? Are we already set in our old habits? During our short stay in Los Angeles, nearly everyone we met questioned why we would live here. I insisted I couldn't leave Texas—I would miss so many things. Bluebonnets. Watering holes. The people. Our friends. Breakfast tacos.

On our first weekend home, Oliver's parents come over for dinner. I get a rotisserie chicken from Central Market and make a simple Mediterranean salad. Vivian will be displeased no matter what, so I do the bare minimum.

Oliver had heard from family friends and a set of cousins in Houston that Allen and Vivian had found out about Dirty Diana and were both crestfallen. We even got a call from the family lawyer asking to meet in person and Oliver was convinced he was being taken out of the will. While we might be moving forward, his parents were still grieving our old selves. We hoped by having them to dinner—maybe finally inviting them to talk to us about their feelings, rather than gossiping to friends—that we could help them to move on.

But the fight we had trained for never materializes. Vivian is cordial and talks about the ravages of her own garden this summer and how no one in Montecito plays cards. Allen wants to hear more about L.A. and then launches into several stories in a row, all set on the golf course. It's a relief when Vivian turns the conversation to Emmy. Oliver and I are so surprised by his parents' good behavior, neither of us tries to raise the subject either. But why are we surprised? This is how Oliver was raised. Better to stay silent than discuss anything real or potentially upsetting. Stuff it deep down inside and move on with a smile on your face. Let it fester, or come out years later as an ulcer, a stroke, or a divorce.

"I wasn't expecting that. But how could I not expect that?" Oliver asks me later.

"It's how they cope," I say, hoping I don't sound flippant.

"That's not how we will."

"It must have been hard. Growing up in that house."

Oliver swallows. "It was fine."

That night, Oliver can't get hard. It's the first time this has ever happened to us. I tell him not to worry, that it's the stress of returning to Rockgate. Oliver turns to me, his face flooded with concern.

"What if it's something more?"

"What is the scariest thing it could be?" I ask, afraid of the answer.

"That we moved too fast. Or maybe Catalina . . ." Catalina. When we left the island we felt invincible. Stronger than ever. But Rockgate has drowned our California glow in harsh fluorescent lighting.

"Should we go back to Miriam?" I ask.

"Do you regret what we did?"

"Not at all. Do you?"

"No," Oliver says and his eyes light up. He takes my hand and presses it against his lips. "We'll get through this. We can't be in therapy for the rest of our lives."

"There's nothing wrong with therapy."

"I know. Therapy brought us together. But it can't hold us together."

We sleep in the guest room, determined to at least be in the same bed. Oliver holds my hand as we fall asleep but halfway through the night he pulls himself out of bed. "I have to do the couch. I'm so sorry. I don't know what is going on."

"Is it me?"

"No. It's my back."

We spend the next few weeks in a confusing mess of sleeping arrangements. We try staying at Oliver's place but Emmy complains about not having the right stuff. We try our room again, the guest room, Oliver back on the couch.

In September, after a particularly sleepless night, I drive Emmy to her first day of school. L'Wren told me that the petition to get us kicked out of St. Mary's had three more signatures, making a total of seven. Not the slam dunk Lorraine was hoping for, but enough to make me nervous.

I decide to park and walk Emmy to her new classroom. I feel like I'm in a teen comedy—a gawky freshman who just slept with the wrong senior, walking down a hallway filled with whispers and stares. Other mothers who would ordinarily stop to ask about my summer are giving me tight smiles instead.

When we reach the open classroom door, Emmy runs inside, grateful not to be holding my sweaty hand any longer.

L'Wren finds me hovering in the doorway. "Keep smiling. It's not that bad."

"Does everyone know?"

"Oh yeah. But there's been a twist."

"In my favor?"

"Yep." L'Wren pauses for effect. "Turns out it was Lorraine's own twelve-year-old son who was giving the blow-job course. Not a fifth-grade girl."

"You're kidding me."

"It literally wrote itself."

"Jesus."

"People want you here, Diana. Penelope's mom told Lorraine to pack her own bag! Or at least she said that's what she *wanted* to tell her."

"I still feel like everyone is staring at me."

"Oh, they are. For sure. But it won't last."

My jaw is tense the entire way back to the parking lot. And then I spot Lorraine, heading toward her Range Rover.

"Hey!" I call out to her. "Lorraine!"

She squares her body to face mine.

"You'll need more than seven signatures to scare me away," I say.

Her expression sours. "Please don't take this personally, Diana. I wouldn't want any family with a mom who produces pornographic material attending our school."

"My job has absolutely nothing to do with you. It doesn't affect you at all."

"But it affects my kids, which is so much worse. Your website is smut. The kids at St. Mary's need role models. How do I explain what you do for a living when my child comes home from a playdate?"

"The more we talk about sex in a healthy way, the less shame our children will feel." I realize I sound like a pamphlet, but it might be the only way she can take it in.

"The women on your website are—"

"Deal with your trauma on someone else's watch. Not on mine. Or my kid's."

I leave Lorraine clutching her actual pearls in the parking lot. I'm sure there will be repercussions, but I'm so blindingly mad I can't find the strength to care.

When I get to my car, my heart sinks at the thought of going into the Monday meeting at Allen's office until I remember I don't have to. It's like waking up from a nightmare, finding yourself cozy in your own bed and realizing you're safe. My body instantly relaxes as I picture the open, airy Dirty Diana offices. And all the people who work there.

When I walk in, Petra, Liam, and Kirby are crowded around the biggest computer screen in the office. Petra FaceTimes Alicia so we can be together and watch as the first fantasy Alicia made goes live.

"You forgot, didn't you?" Liam asks.

"No. Just school stuff. That other mom and I are still in a . . . disagreement."

"Why are you wasting your time trying to convince some dreadful woman of anything?" Petra asks.

"I'm not anymore."

"I know you weren't sure about this," Liam says to me, nervously. "Initially."

"I've come around."

"No pun intended."

Kirby pokes him in the ribs. "Just say thank you!"

"Thank you. For trusting me. And the listeners. And the projections. And the basic, essential rules of turning a profit. Shit—am I my father?"

"It's up!" Petra claps her hands together. "People can watch!"

The video begins with an extreme close-up of our lead actress, Maya, speaking directly into the lens. "My fantasy is . . ."

The film Alicia made is somehow both playful and sexy. A series of beautifully lit portraits of Maya in various settings, frozen at first like a painting, and then doing simple everyday things, narrating her fantasy as it becomes increasingly erotic.

The first comments pour in: Beyond hot. Finally, something for me. Trina's fantasy next? Please! When will the next one be avail?

"Alicia! You did it."

She beams. "So many babies are going to be made because of me."

...

On the drive home, I replay Liam's forecast of our numbers doubling, and Petra's bright smile, "See?"

I don't want to stick around long enough for her to tell me it's her last day in the office. I prefer a Jasper-style Irish exit, and then one day I'll come in and I won't smell her perfume or hear her voice calling to me excitedly from her office, "Diana!"

So I slipped away to my office then snuck off for home.

When I arrive, my excitement over the launch fades—Emmy is still at school and Oliver is ensconced in our sunken couch. I extend my hand and pull him to me. "It's not us, Oliver," I say, with absolute clarity. "It's the house."

Chapter Seventeen

It's Liam's megawatt smile that makes every guest at the wedding tear up. And Kirby's sweet, doleful eyes. She's stunning. Her dress is bigger than she is but she does not let it swallow her up. She glides across the dance floor like a princess with just a touch of a villainess, the kind you root for. With a boom mic at her side.

"You'll thank me later," she tells me when I take it off her hands. "We might have a wedding fantasy one day and we'll need some background."

I find L'Wren at the backyard bar. "Everything is beautiful . . ." Her voice trails off.

"L'Wren."

"I'm just saying, if they had used my planner, she would have never let that violinist wear jeans. Even if it is a dark wash. It wouldn't have been a conversation."

Liam and Kirby proudly paid for every cent of the ceremony, mostly thanks to the subscription bump we've enjoyed from posting video as well. And the biggest wedding gift on the table is from Petra. She sent it from Morocco, along with a postcard for us all:

Please tell the newlyweds to extend their honeymoon and visit me here. Please tell L'Wren there are stray cats everywhere, and I've already adopted two! I'm a cat lady now. Please tell Alicia there is no such thing as "quiet" in Marrakesh but she'll fall in love with the place anyway. And Diana . . . the Ziploc baggie is finally empty but my heart is so, so full. Love, P.

P.S. Have we thought about Dirty Diana lube? There's the most fragrant pomegranate tree in my yard. . . . It should smell just like that. One of you get on that! xoxo

Arthur steals L'Wren for a dance. Oliver takes my hand and we follow, and the late-October evening swirls from there. Cake and champagne toasts and Liam's and Kirby's beaming smiles. After seeing off the newlyweds, Oliver and I get in our car and begin my favorite part of the night: our drive home. It was exactly two months ago that I pulled Oliver from the couch and drove him to the site of his work-in-progress house, the one with the tree growing in it and the sleepy birch out front.

"I don't know how we do it. But this is our house."

"You want to live here?" he asked.

"There are too many sad memories where we are now. They're closing in on us."

"It's farther from Emmy's school. . . . And the frontage road is terrible when it rains but . . ." Oliver made a slow circle around the empty house, still unfinished. "You want to hear something strange? There is a big part of me that's always been building this house for us. Even when there was no 'us.' I hoped, even then."

We moved in before there was a kitchen and with some of the floors still ripped up. The three of us shared a crumbling bathroom with a cold shower until the water heater could be replaced. In sour moods, Emmy complained; in good moods she told us she loved camping and talked us into s'mores for lunch.

I called Allison Kidd and said no to the movie and to the money. The idea of putting out a different version of myself now that Dirty Diana is finally out there felt about as appealing as taking back my old job at Allen's firm. Natalie understood. She told me there are so many different versions of her out in the world she has had to accept it but she's never liked it.

Oliver and I make love in various rooms. And sometimes we don't. We've taken the pressure off except to tell each other even the most insignificant parts of our day, just to stay in the habit.

And by the time the article came out in *Vogue*, I'd nearly forgotten about it. When it finally ran, they skipped the Q&A altogether and to my surprise, only printed my fantasy.

I'm on a city sidewalk, beneath the shadow of a skyscraper. You're beside me. I think it's you. Your profile is familiar, with your perfectly straight nose and full, rosy lips. Only no matter how long I stare, you don't turn my way, so I can't see your entire face. But it has to be you.

I don't recognize your clothes. You're in a suit, crisp and tailored. Its gray linen matches the skyscraper, sleek and modern, all glass and steel. Did you plan it this way? Why would you? I feel the sudden urge to slip my hand beneath your jacket, under your shirt, and run my fingers across your bare skin. But what if it's not you?

We don't enter the building right away. All around us, hordes of people hurry in and out. A broad-shouldered man in a fedora comes through the revolving door and bumps into me, hard. I turn to protest but his dimples are disarming and his brown eyes are warm and apologetic peeking out under his dark lashes, so I smile to say it's okay and he disappears into the crowd.

"Let's go," you say. Your voice is hoarse but gentle. It has to be you. When I steal another glance, you turn away.

We enter the lobby and the place shifts. The security desk evaporates. So do all the people swirling around us. The giant bank of elevators with their endless dinging sounds are gone too. The walls close in and the lobby shrinks and it's just you and me.

We're on the ground floor of an apartment building. An aging lobby with a row of mailboxes and a tired velvet settee for waiting. There's an elevator so old-fashioned that I expect when it opens it'll have its own ancient operator inside.

"Is this where you live?" I ask, a thrill running up my spine. I want you to take me to your place so we can be alone. I reach for your hand but you tell me, "Not yet."

The narrow elevator doors open. It's small inside, but there are mirrors on each wall to give us the illusion of more space.

Finally, I see your face in their reflection. It is you. But it's disorientating. You're different in every mirror. Your face is sometimes unshaven, sometimes smooth. You're wearing a T-shirt; an oxford; no shirt at all.

You turn to me and grin, your blue-green eyes full of mischief. "They're meant to be a distraction. All the mirrors." Like a Kusama exhibit of infinity mirrors. Light-years. We're here, but swallowed up.

You step toward me. My pulse quickens. You finger the straps of my dress. I look down at myself for the first time. It's the same dress I was wearing the first time we met. When you showed me that terrible apartment and we couldn't keep our eyes off each other. The dress is plain and rumpled and nothing like the suit you're wearing.

As if reading my mind you say, "It's perfect," and nod to the mirrors. I'm in a green silk gown; a blue sweater; a black dress.

You kiss my shoulder and slip one strap off, and then the next. The dress slips from my chest and catches at my hips. You close the gap between us and the heat from your body warms mine.

My chin tilts to meet yours. Your lips are soft but the kiss is urgent. The elevator begins to move. A rush of anticipation. We're one step closer to your place.

You don't stop at the kiss. You push me against the wall and press your body into mine but I still feel like I'm falling. Even though you're solid and strong and I can feel your excitement build.

The elevator slows near the third floor.

You lift the hem of my dress but I grab you by the wrist. "What if someone gets on?"

"Who cares?" Your breath is warm on my neck. I lean back so you can kiss every inch of it.

The doors open and I freeze. But no one is there. I relax again. I let your hands roam everywhere. Down my stomach, up my thighs. I watch us in the mirrors—for a moment, every reflection is the same: you moving against me, my legs around your torso, my hands in your hair. I slip off your jacket. Unbutton your shirt. I want to see more of you in the mirror and I know we have to move quickly. I look up to the ceiling and the infinity mirror breaks into a hundred different images.

It's you, planting zinnias in the front yard.

It's us, alone in a stairwell, me in your lap.

We're inviting him into our hotel room.

Slipping away from a party.

A million different versions of who we were and who we still can be.

The elevator nears the final floor. "This is us," you say and pull me to my feet.

I bend to pick up our discarded clothes.

"Leave them. When we get inside"—you pull me close—"I'd like to tie you to the bathroom sink." I smile. You tie me to the sink in the

evening and drive carpool in the morning. Why not? My fantasy is saying yes. To you, to me, to pleasure.

The elevator jerks to a stop. My eyes fly open.

I'm alone in our bed, but I can hear you down the hall, the familiar sounds of you moving through our house.

Luckily, I'm awake now.

Acknowledgments

Thank you to our readers for coming on this journey with us. We are incredibly grateful.

PHOTO: CHRISTOPHER ZEBO

PHOTO: SYDNEY SHEEHAN

Lifelong best friends JEN BESSER and SHANA FESTE met as eleven-year-olds in California and have been collaborating ever since. *Dirty Diana,* first launched as a podcast starring Demi Moore, debuted at #1 on Apple, was nominated for Podcast of the Year and won the Ambie for Best Fiction, Screenwriting. Shana is the award-winning screenwriter and director of several feature films, including *Country Strong* and *Run Sweetheart Run.* Jen is a fiction editor and publisher. They now live thousands of miles apart and talk every day.

About the Type

This book was set in Dante, a typeface designed by Giovanni Mardersteig (1892–1977). Conceived as a private type for the Officina Bodoni in Verona, Italy, Dante was originally cut only for hand composition by Charles Malin, the famous Parisian punch cutter, between 1946 and 1952. Its first use was in an edition of Boccaccio's *Trattatello in laude di Dante* that appeared in 1954. The Monotype Corporation's version of Dante followed in 1957. Though modeled on the Aldine type used for Pietro Cardinal Bembo's treatise De Aetna in 1495, Dante is a thoroughly modern interpretation of that venerable face.

Books Driven by the Heart

Sign up for our newsletter
and find more you'll love:

thedialpress.com

@THEDIALPRESS

@THEDIALPRESS

Penguin Random House collects and processes your
personal information. See our Notice at Collection
and Privacy Policy at prh.com/notice.